Myopia

Jeff Gardiner

CROOKED
CAT

Discover us online:
www.crookedcatpublishing.com

Join us on facebook:
www.facebook.com/crookedcatpublishing

For
Janet and Gerald Gardiner,
my Mum and Dad.
Thanks for your endless
love and support.

About the Author

Jeff Gardiner was born in Jos, Nigeria, although his formative teenage years were spent in West London. Now living in Crawley, West Sussex with his wife and two children, he teaches Drama, English and Film Studies in a secondary comprehensive school. He enjoys listening to rock music and is even willing to confess to having a passion for progressive rock. His favourite authors include Mervyn Peake, Graham Joyce and Haruki Murakami.

His first writing achievement came with an adaptation of his MPhil thesis, The Age of Chaos: the Multiverse of Michael Moorcock which has recently been expanded and revised in preparation for republication, now retitled The Law of Chaos.
Jeff has already enjoyed success with his short stories. His collection A Glimpse of the Numinous containing horror, slipstream and humour, has been described as: "genuinely fascinating, weird and original". Many of his stories have appeared in magazines, such as Twisted Tongue and Estronomicon; on websites such as www.raphaelsvillage.com, and in anthologies, such as the award-winning The Elastic Book of Numbers.

Myopia is his first novel. Jeff is currently writing a work of fiction set in Nigeria during the Biafran war, as well as preparing another novel for teenagers. For more information visit his website and blog at **www.jeffgardiner.com**

Acknowledgements

Thanks to Laurence Patterson and Sue McCaskill for their expertise and editing skills.

And to Sandy for her patience and encouragement.

Love and hugs to Emily and Bethany for all the laughter we share, which brings me so much joy.

Jeff Gardiner
December 2012

Myopia

Chapter One

"Here comes four-eyes."

"What, that speccy git in our technology group?"

"Yeah. Oi! Goggles! Where'd you get the space visors from? NASA?" Cruel sniggering filled the corridor.

As Jerry looked up his glasses slipped down his nose, so all he could see was a fuzzy mix of shapes and colours. He wrinkled his nose to lift his glasses back into his sightline but then remembered how it made him look haughty, so he prodded the central frame with his forefinger to slide his glasses back up his nose. Now he made out a double line of pupils, mostly from his year, making a tunnel leading to the outside door to the field. It looked like the rows guests make when a newly married couple leave their wedding reception, only Jerry didn't think there would be as much jollity – or kissing.

This gang, made up of boys and girls, often stood here, threatening younger pupils who made the mistake of walking past. He knew he should be worried.

"Oi, you four-eyed freak."

One of the boys grabbed his blazer. Jerry let himself go limp. He'd been in this situation before.

"I'm talking to you, dickhead."

Jerry knew the speaker only too well: Wayno. Their noses almost touched. Wayno's breath reeked and Jerry guessed brushing teeth was not a priority for him.

He wanted to walk away but Wayno held him tightly. Where were the bloody teachers when you wanted them?

Always there when you don't need them.

Wayno suddenly let go but Jerry felt himself tugged backwards until he stumbled into the corner under the staircase, surrounded by about half a dozen boys and a few girls. He was now being manhandled by a different boy known as Rhino, Wayno's bodyguard.

"On the way to the library are you, you boff?"

The library was actually in the opposite direction but Jerry guessed this wasn't the time to be pedantic.

"Are you gonna answer or what?" Rhino snarled, spitting as he spoke. A fleck of saliva landed on Jerry's cheek. His eyes flicked quickly between the framed limits of his focal range. As he began sweating he felt his glasses slip back down his nose. Too scared to push them back, he maintained his silence, glad the marauding bullies stood before him in a blur.

Before he knew it a hand appeared in front of his face but not with the velocity he imagined. Instead the hand hovered at Jerry's eye-level, tilted with fingers pointed towards him. Then suddenly some fingernails clicked against the lenses of Jerry's glasses.

"Pretty useful in a fight these visors," said Wayno. "I can't poke your eyes out – so I'll just have to rip your whole head off."

Many responses flashed through Jerry's mind but he sensibly kept his mouth shut. It meant his tormentors assumed him stupid or easy prey but saying the words out loud would only earn him a visit to intensive care.

Suddenly his whole world fuzzed into a kaleidoscope of blurs as Wayno removed his glasses, leaving Jerry standing in a lonely world of short-sightedness. He could no longer see the bullies at all; not even sure any more of his location in school, having lost all visual markers normally putting things into context.

The crowd around him became unidentifiable blobs – weird creatures continually contorting, ebbing and flowing. It was impossible to see where one of them began and another ended; they all just merged into an insignificant mass of blobbiness. Jerry imagined them as one giant monster made of snot, which made him smile.

Although he couldn't focus on faces he became aware of movements. Voices murmured, overlapped and buzzed but Jerry chose not to listen, preferring his own thoughts as he blocked out the world around him.

Where the hell were those stupid teachers?

Jerry hoped silence and inertia would bore the bullies into giving up. Although the theory sounded good it never worked in practice. Responding didn't work: it just made them more determined to hurt you. Ignoring didn't work either. Jerry had already learnt that bullies were angry individuals who couldn't be reasoned with. Whatever he did would be wrong, so doing nothing and conserving his energy and sanity appeared the best policy.

What they did to his glasses concerned him most. Please don't break them, he pleaded silently. He didn't have a spare pair.

"You're a sad little swat aren't you?" Wayno's voice rudely interrupted Jerry's thoughts.

Not really, thought Jerry. He was mainly in middle groups and didn't do any more work than most. Just because he didn't hang around with Wayno's gang and do what he said, they had to find some stereotype to label him with.

"What a little mummy's boy," Wayno teased, slapping Jerry on both cheeks. As Wayno's face got closer, Jerry realised his tormentor was wearing his glasses.

"God, your eyes are bad. You could do welding in these." The inane giggling from the others encouraged their leader, who started to perform to his audience. "These speccies are thicker than magnifying glasses." After another round of titters and sniggers, Wayno's voice became aggressive.

"Say after me, four-eyes, 'I'm a little saddo'. It's not hard."

"Yeah, but you are, eh, Wayno," chipped in one of Wayno's toadies. "Rock hard."

What a snivelling little brown-nose, thought Jerry.

Jerry stuck to his silence and hung on for dear life. It would all be over soon: surely the bell should go any minute now.

Jerry guessed Wayno would hate 'losing face' in front of his cronies. Wayno – snorting and still wearing Jerry's glasses – leaned right in to Jerry until their noses touched.

"You're bloody dead, mate. D'you hear?" Wayno head-butted Jerry with some force, ripped off the glasses and then punched his victim hard in the stomach. Jerry wanted to fall over, but Wayno's mates held him up.

"Debag him," Wayno ordered with a gesture, before striding away like some mafia Don, content for others do his dirty work.

Jerry felt his trousers and underpants being whipped down to his feet – probably by Rhino – whilst his hands were held. Screams of laughter erupted in the corridors, echoing up the stairwell. By the sound of it quite a crowd gathered to witness his humiliation. Eventually, his arms were freed, allowing him to double over and collapse. Jerry managed to pull his trousers back up swiftly then do up his button and zip before attending to his aching head and burning midriff. With his head throbbing he got on all fours and scrabbled about for his glasses. He patted the filthy floor in all directions. The corner had been quickly vacated by the crowd and Jerry patiently swept both hands to and fro with no luck. Still not having found them when the bell rang, Jerry cursed his short-sightedness.

Lots of pupils rushed past him and he wanted to scream for them to stop, fearing his glasses would be crushed underfoot. Couldn't they see he needed help? Jerry wanted to cry when he remembered the pain in his head and belly, but he refused to do so. Crying really was not the done thing in school – especially not for a boy.

"Are you okay, Jerry?" He heard a female voice above him but couldn't identify the speaker. Her voice sounded kind and at first he thought it might be a teacher or one of the office ladies. A hand took firm hold of his and hauled him up. Close up, he vaguely recognised Parminder Sidhu. She sat near him in English and he knew her immediately as he screwed up his eyes and smiled. He could just make out her long, black, glossy hair; nut-brown eyes and cheeks which dimpled when she smiled. Right now her huge eyes stared into his in genuine concern.

"Okay, mate?" Parminder dusted the right arm of his blazer still grey with muck and fluff. "Shall I take you to the office?"

"No … no thanks. I'm fine. I just need to find my glasses."

Before he knew it, she fell on her hands and knees.

"Here we go," she said, jumping nimbly back to her feet and patting her stockinged knees. "They've seen better days, I think."

Gratefully accepting the wire frames Jerry inspected them carefully. One arm now bent completely the wrong way and both lenses were badly scratched. In fact one lens looked cracked beyond repair. He'd have to carry on now with just one eye.

"Thanks Parminder," Jerry said weakly.

"I prefer Mindy," she replied, rewarding him with her dimpled smile.

He realised this might be the first time he'd properly spoken to her and he wished it could have been under better circumstances. He could only hope she hadn't been there earlier to witness his public exposure. "I'm fine. Really. Thanks … Mindy."

"Well, you take care, hun." Mindy strolled out of his range of vision.

His misery reached completion when he put on his glasses.

Jerry could see nothing out of the left eye except fog and a cracked line across the middle of the lens. The view through the right lens appeared slightly better although a few scratches to one side gave a kind of starburst effect when looking at light. Taking them off to inspect them, Jerry peered closely at each lens and saw white lines etched onto the transparent plastic as well as smears and blobs; they needed a thorough clean. Well, it could be worse, he considered.

Huffing loudly over each lens, Jerry then tugged his shirt out from his trousers to use the hem as a polishing cloth. This only smeared the dirt making them even harder to look through. He needed the special spray and soft material in his cupboard at home. After several rubs they became vaguely translucent. A small clear gap meant he could see through a small round window in the right lens. That would have to do for now.

With the bell having gone ages ago, it left him late for Science. Head down, he ran to his locker, grabbed his Science books and pencil case then sprinted along the playground, through the double doors and up the stairs to Lab 5.

"Hough! You're late. Stay behind at the end. And tuck your shirt in – it looks like you're wearing a skirt. What are you? A girl?"

The whole class laughed as Jerry prodded his shirt into his trousers then sat down.

What a crap day this was turning out to be.

Chapter Two

After lunch came tutor time, which basically involved twenty-eight students piling in to a run-down mobile classroom, screaming and sitting on desks, while Miss Powys attempted to tick off names. As soon as the second bell went they all disappeared whether she'd completed the register or not, and without a word being emitted by the tutor. She'd given up attempting to control them in year 8, having tried being friendly; being strict; bribing; shouting; humour; sarcasm and emotional blackmail. Her last hope had been that the girls might view her as an older sister and the boys might fancy her in her tight, low tops. None of these tactics worked. Notices and messages put in her register by the office or other members of staff remained unread, so nobody in her tutor group attended clubs or extra-curricular activities. Miss Powys came to the conclusion it wasn't worth her health or sanity, and so now saw registration of S10 as something to survive: to get through unscathed.

With the rest of S10 gone, Jerry ambled up to the front desk hopefully.

"Miss – I want to report some bullying ..."

"Oh, Jerry, I really don't have time for this right now. I have to get to my lesson. I tell you what – you go down to the school office and ask for an incident form. Fill it in and give it to Mr Platt. Okay?" Miss Powys looked at her watch and grabbed her bag. "Oh, and as you're going that way anyway could you take the register for me? Ta." And with that she swept out.

Jerry's heart sank. Mr Platt was his Head of Year. All year 10 pupils laughed at the prospect of being sent to Mr Platt. If you were sent for discipline you could breathe a sigh of relief as he would only end up giving you a lecture, during which you could switch off, and then be cautioned with an empty threat of getting your parents in. With Mr Platt you had to look sorry, promise never to do it again and you'd be off and away.

If you went to report something you knew it to be a futile endeavour. If he'd been a year older then he would report to Miss Harvey – definitely a woman of action. She would do anything to help bring bullies to justice. Miscreants in year 11 trembled at the thought of being sent to Miss Harvey. But he must report to Mr Platt and he didn't feel too hopeful. Still it gave him good cause to miss the beginning of Geography.

Once he'd obtained an incident form from the kind Mrs Billington in reception, he made his way to the office of his Head of Year.

"Come in."

Jerry leant on the handle and pushed the door inwards. Mr Platt sat with his back to Jerry, head down, scribbling furiously at his desk. Shutting the door carefully behind him, Jerry stood patiently, waiting for the teacher to stop writing; any minute now a natural break or convenient moment should occur when Mr Platt would stop and look up.

And he waited …

It seemed bad manners to interrupt an important adult very clearly hard at work, and Jerry wondered if he should just creep away and leave it. Instead, he decided to clear his throat loudly and hope it wouldn't be deemed disrespectful. Mr Platt's head flicked round at the sound and he must have caught sight of Jerry's shoes, as his eye-line never raised above ground level.

"Mmm. Yes?"

Jerry expected Mr Platt to spin round and offer him a seat, but it seemed he must talk to his back as the Head of Year returned to his writing.

"I've come to report an incident," Jerry stated clearly.

"What sort of incident?" Scribble, scribble, scribble.

"Um … bullying, sir."

"Now then, young man," Mr Platt stopped writing but kept his back to Jerry. "You know the school has a zero-tolerance approach to bullying and we will not allow defiance to infect the foundation and infrastructure of this institution. You know the rules and yet you dare to …"

"No sir, sorry, but I have been bullied," Jerry raised his voice to interrupt this inanity.

"Ah, right … I see." Mr Platt finally turned round and grabbed an official form from one of the pigeon holes on the wall, conveniently within arm's reach from his swivel chair. "And you are?"

Blimey, thought Jerry. You've been my Head of Year for over three years, yet still have no idea who I am. He toyed with the idea of making up a name just to see what would happen.

"Jerry Hough, sir."

"Hough?" it clearly meant nothing to him. Jerry felt depressed by the realisation that he was one of the invisibles in school: not naughty enough but also not quite clever enough to make his mark above the rest; one of the grey folk who slipped through the middle. How embarrassing.

"A bullying issue should be dealt with by Mr Finn." Mr Platt pushed the form towards Jerry. "Fill in this incident form and take it to Mr Finn."

Jerry thought he should explain how he had already obtained a form, but kept it to himself. Two is always better than one. The prospect of seeing Mr Finn made him feel more hopeful. Mr Q Finn was always willing to help, and, as Deputy Head, he cut an imposing figure – about six foot five and with a very pointed chin. Everyone assumed the Q stood for Quentin as it fitted his character; but when the staff suddenly took to wearing security badges with their full names, it came to light that the Q actually stood for Quincy. Then last year he turned into Mr Quincy Finn OBE, for his tireless work for charity and the community.

Unsure whether to say thanks or apologise for time-wasting, Jerry took the form and trudged towards the door. Before exiting the office he considered bowing with a sarcastic flourish, or even sticking up two fingers. It wouldn't have mattered if he'd done both because Mr Platt sat with his back to him again now, having returned to his psychotic scribbling as if Jerry never existed.

The prospect of seeing Mr Finn became an entirely different matter. Jerry sat patiently outside his office trying to fill in one of the incident forms, which proved to be more difficult than it first appeared. Name and date were easy enough, but when it came to describing 'the nature of the incident' he began to struggle.

"I was walking innocently down the corridor," he began to write, "when I was accosted…" (no hang on – accosted? No-one writes that. What does it mean anyway? Jerry crossed the word out) … "threatened by a large …" (massive? huge?) … "group of pupils." (Should he specify a number? Or write "boys"? He preferred not to mention that some of the bullies were girls). "I was stopped by the doors near room 42 and they called me names – particularly referring to my glasses." (Should he quote some of the names used? He remembered "dickhead".)

Then Jerry reached the quandary regarding whether he should 'grass-up' Wayno and Rhino at all and risk their vengeful wrath. This remained the ultimate paradox – a major problem for any victim of bullying. Should he tell all and sod the inevitable retaliation, or should he take the law into his own hands? The only other option was to keep quiet and hope the bully gets bored and goes away, perhaps even respecting the fact the victim hasn't dobbed him or her in.

As Jerry juggled these thoughts in his head and whilst

worrying about how to explain his debagging on the form, Quincy Finn stepped out of his office in a sprightly manner.

"Jerry is it?"

Smiling and nodding, Jerry felt a sense of relief that someone important in school knew his name. On the other hand Quincy possessed an awesome photographic memory; his brain was a computer memorising every single detail, fact, figure and statistic required for running the school – which he seemed to do more than the Head. It always seemed odd to Jerry to think Quincy had been a PE teacher, although apparently he once played basketball for England. Now he just taught RS to years 7 and 8.

"Yes sir, Jerry Hough, sir."

"Come in, come in. Sit ye down. What can I do you for?"

Unsure whether this counted as a joke (Quincy wasn't laughing) or whether this giant of a man just derived a great deal of pleasure from scaring children, Jerry sat down and tried to stop blinking uncontrollably. Aware again of his damaged glasses, his right eye darted to the small window through the lens which afforded him a restricted view of the world.

"I want to report an incident of bullying … I mean I have been bullied, sir. I saw Mr Platt and he told me to see you, sir."

"Did he now? Did he indeed?" Quincy Finn sat down, but even in a seated position with his long limbs dangling in all directions, he still seemed to take up most of his office. Jerry took a deep breath in, trying to occupy the least amount of space he could in his little corner.

"Tell me all about it, Jerry. I want you to be assured we will not tolerate any kind of bullying in this fine academic institution. We take all accusations very seriously and the person who did this to you will be severely punished. You're not alone – we are all here to listen and to support you. Do you understand?"

Jerry nodded.

"I feel moved to add here that you are also never alone, Jerry. Whilst you do have parents, family, teachers and friends who remain an active network of support, it is worth remembering, Jerry, in those lonely, frightening moments in the early hours of the morning when you're lying awake in bed tossing and turning…"

Jerry looked up bemused, but of course stayed silent.

"…there is one who holds you in his loving arms. He cradles you, comforts you and whispers in your ear." And Mr Finn actually leaned in close to Jerry and whispered: "I love you, my child. You are mine. Don't be afraid. Trust me and enter into my eternal bliss."

It struck Jerry that if a social worker had popped a head round the door at this very moment and heard the Deputy Head's whisper, then Quincy Finn would be reported, sacked, put on a list and attacked by a mob of bigoted tabloid readers. However, Jerry liked to think himself more sophisticated than to laugh at someone who used the word 'tossing' correctly; and he knew damn well Quincy didn't fancy him, so he expelled these puerile thoughts.

In actual fact, QF was being very kind by offering him the love, hope and security that faith in God brought to millions of people. There were times when Jerry did indeed lie awake at night wondering what the hell (perhaps not such an appropriate term in these circumstances) love, life and existence were all about.

"Let me pray for you Jerry."

Not being a church-goer, Jerry felt uncomfortable if a little intrigued. As a child his Granny said prayers when putting him to bed and Quincy Finn always ended assemblies with a prayer – being the only teacher to do so.

"Lord we just want to lift up your holy name and ask your spirit to come down upon us."

Jerry looked at Mr Finn who closed his eyes and held one hand up with fingers splayed. Wondering whether to do the

14

same, or put his hands together like his Granny taught him, he decided in the end to just look down into his lap.

"Bless Jerry here in his plight," Quincy Finn continued with a deep intonation. "Give him a feeling of confidence so he can face his persecutors with his head held high. Be with him so he knows your love and wisdom. Help him to respond in the best way without anger or hatred, but so he can continue to become the best person he can. Let this bullying stop, Lord. Send your spirit on to these bullies and let them see with shame what misery and torment they are creating. We put this problem into your hands, Lord. Amen."

Jerry made a guttural sound which he meant as 'Amen' but sounded more like clearing his throat. In actual fact Jerry felt a lot better. He knew Mr Finn meant well, doing what he thought best, but he felt a tad sceptical that one prayer would bring about an end to the bullying.

However, one thing old Quincy said in his prayer struck Jerry: he said about responding "without anger or hatred", which made sense to Jerry. A bully only wants you to get scared or angry, so it made sense not to show either. And if you hate the bully back then you become just as bad as the bully. He knew that many victims just went on to bully other, smaller kids, but Jerry refused to become another statistic or stereotype. He fervently believed the chain of bullying must end with him. Thus he should not feel hatred or anger.

"Now then Jerry," Mr Finn said, reaching over to an in-tray on his desk and tweaking out a piece of paper containing very familiar grids and line-spacing. "I need you to fill in an incident form, and this issue really needs to be dealt with by your Head of Year. Mr Platt really must learn to deal with these things himself. It is, after all, part of his job description." Jerry detected more than a little tension in his voice. "I shall email him to make sure he keeps me in the loop," Mr Finn continued. "Good luck young man and God bless."

So with three incident forms in his possession Jerry left the

Deputy Head's office confused. The prayer had been unexpected if strangely helpful; he did feel a little less anxious now. However, the prospect of returning to Mr Platt filled him with a sense of complete hopelessness, so he decided not to bother.

A check of his watch confirmed that half an hour still remained of Geography. It seemed pointless going in half-way through – he'd only have to explain in front of everyone where he'd been and why. No doubt some of the pupils in there had been witnesses to his debagging and he'd never hear the end of it. A much better use of his time would be to go home and do his homework.

It amazed him how easily he could slip out of school. He walked past the Head's office and down the corridor by the hall. He knew if he used the further door then he could get outside without going past reception where Mrs Bilington would ask awkward questions before he hit the door-release button. The side door allowed him to walk around the technology workshops and down a small avenue of trees to the wide open front gates. From there five swift strides took him round the corner and out of sight.

As he turned the corner he heard a raised female voice.

"Oh, that's right ... typical bloke – running away ..."

Jerry wondered initially if this comment was aimed at him. He kept walking and saw a figure ahead with her back to him talking into a mobile whilst vigorously brandishing a cigarette in her other hand. As his bus stop lay further up on the same side of the road he felt forced to walk past her.

"Yes, the test was positive ... Of course it's yours. What, you calling me a slag?"

Just then she turned round and he instantly recognised Miss Powys, his form tutor.

Startled by Jerry's presence, she quickly hid the cigarette behind her back and snapped her phone shut.

"You never heard a thing okay?" Miss Powys snarled waving

her fag in front of his face before realising her mistake and flicking it into the road.

Jerry shook his head solemnly.

"One word and you'll be doing detentions for the rest of your life, you understand? You keep quiet about this and I say nothing about you bunking off. Agreed?"

Jerry nodded. "I never saw you, miss."

The relief on Miss Powys' face was palpable.

"Good lad."

Jerry walked on and peeked quickly behind him to see Miss Powys deftly lighting up another cigarette whilst dialling her phone. Then the number 17 bus appeared and Jerry ran whilst fumbling for his bus pass.

Chapter Three

Once home, Jerry decided to be conscientious and get on with his homework. He knew he had Maths and Art both due the next day and in that order. Not doing Maths homework equalled writing a suicide note. Old Haddock (real name Haydock) shouted when happy; making him angry just involved turning up the volume. 'Intense bawling' seemed to be his default setting. Having made the mistake once of not completing his homework, Jerry girded his loins and opened the text book to page 97: 'Quadratic Equations'. Whilst he could vaguely follow the logic of the formula, he knew any query to Old Haddock about what it meant would meet with a bellowed reply to stop asking stupid questions.

So he completed the work certain all the answers were correct without really understanding its purpose. He guessed it just involved passing exams, which seemed to be the point of education: to learn inexplicable things and get grades which got you a better job than some other people.

The art homework proved problematic in a different way. He liked his Art teacher – Mrs Benson - whose calm but firm way with all pupils made her genuinely popular. Without needing to shout, she dealt with defiant students in an efficient, stealthy way; never having to raise her voice. The homework was "to draw a familiar object from an unusual perspective, in the manner of surrealism or expressionism". Mrs Benson seemed determined to make them all appreciate the art of Dali and Van Gogh and be generally inspired by these masters. Mrs Benson kept telling the class how madness and genius overlapped until it sometimes became impossible to see the difference.

Draw an everyday object in an unusual way. Dali seemed to enjoy painting exploding giraffes and things propped up on crutches on the beach, whilst Van Gogh just used extremely bright colours and painted like a nine year old. Jerry thought his own attempt at painting sunflowers at the age of nine far better, but sadly he failed to sell his canvas for millions of pounds. There's no accounting for taste.

As Jerry looked about him for an everyday object to draw he got irritated by the distracting scratches on his glasses creating beams of light across his vision. When he closed his right eye the damaged lens made everything cloudy, warped and certainly unusual. Moving his head from left to right then opening and closing each eye in turn did give him a new perspective on such familiar surroundings – in fact it made objects shift from side to side. Jerry got up and wandered into the kitchen, which probably contained the most familiar objects and saw the array of items before him: kettle, microwave, sink, cupboards, bottles, iron, bananas, spice rack, saucepans, kitchen roll, cups, spoons hanging up – perfect.

Once he'd chosen a particular view he grabbed a nearby pine stool and sat with the sketch pad on his knee. Then the clever bit: Jerry slowly removed his glasses as if taking off a blindfold to see his location for the first time. All the familiar items blurred into each other. The light glared and flickered off saucepans, cutlery and the kettle making them particularly stand out. Jerry suddenly became more aware of shades and colours rather than distinct shapes. The details and writing were out of focus and some things were just a mush of lumpiness. He knew over there should be the draining board full of cups, plates and pans, but it now seemed more like a multicoloured … as he stared at the shape, he could see what looked like a horn or antenna. He knew it to be the handle of a saucepan, but enjoyed the game. The round bowl to the left of it could be a giant snail's shell or perhaps the whole thing could be a slightly deformed rhinoceros. But as he shifted position slightly, Jerry saw it exactly: the silhouette of a seated unicorn right here in his own kitchen. The handle was the horn. Those bowls became its head and curled up body. Two knives even stuck up like ears. The more he looked the more convinced he became by his own illusion until he felt a little spooked.

And so his Art homework developed on the paper. His actual draftsmanship left a little to be desired, but he felt pleased with the idea and even thought up a name for his own masterpiece: 'Welcome To My World'.

By the time his mum got home from work Jerry felt pleased with himself for completing all his homework.

"Hello, my darling," Mrs Hough called out as she hung her coat on the peg behind the utility room door. "Good day at school?"

"Yes, thanks."

She appeared in the front room smiling. Her skirt suit made her look neat and tidy whilst her dyed blonde hair made her look younger than forty-five by covering up the rapidly multiplying grey hairs. Mrs Hough also wore trendy rectangular glasses to correct her long-sightedness. He often heard his mum say as people get older they tend to grow long-sighted and so he continued to hope getting older would correct his short-sightedness. By the age of fifty he'd have 20-20 vision.

Helping his mum cut up vegetables for dinner was now a regular routine, so Jerry peeled and sliced the carrots whilst Mrs Hough cubed the spuds. Once completed she took her son's hand and pulled him in for a cuddle.

"Don't say you're too old for this. I need a hug."

Secretly Jerry enjoyed hugging his mum, something too uncool to admit out loud. His dad always scolded her for it.

"You'll turn him into a softie, you daft bat", he would say.

So Jerry embraced his mum who kissed him on the forehead.

"What happened to your glasses?"

Never try to hide things from your mum, thought Jerry. Eyes like a hawk.

"Fell over playing football," he lied effortlessly. "Such a great tackle, but the ol' specs flew off and scraped along the ground. Then one of the lads accidently trod on them. They're a bit bent and scratched but I can still see okay…"

Mrs Hough reached out and removed them, inspecting the lenses from every angle.

"…sort of …" Jerry added.

"I'm surprised you can see anything. Oh, Jerry, they're ruined." His mum handed them back with a look of disappointment. "We'll have to get some new ones – maybe tomorrow before tea we could drive in to the opticians. Your dad'll be late home anyway. Don't let me forget will you?"

His dad appeared just as Jerry finished laying the table. Mr Hough came home grumpy most evenings. He worked as a tree-surgeon, managing a gang of five other men, cutting and pruning trees for the local council. It was tough and hefty work. Before even saying hello he changed into his Crawley FC football top and collected a beer from the fridge. After dinner he poured himself another beer and settled into his chair to watch the punters' pre-amble and build-up before the match whilst the other two cleared away and did the washing up. Finally Jerry settled down too, squinting at the telly through his one good eye.

In the first half both Crawley Town and their Portuguese opposition played cautiously and with little spark, causing Jerry's dad to hurl a string of shouted obscenities at the television. "Bunch of pansies! Bloody disgrace!"

No changes were made for the second half but Crawley came out with a greater sense of attacking purpose, using their wingers to great effect. When they missed an open goal Jerry's dad went apoplectic.

"Oh you donkey! You dickhead!" Mr Hough screamed. Jerry remembered that same name being applied to him earlier that day.

The rest of the game remained a stalemate, with nobody really looking like breaking down the other's defence. Mr Hough began to snore on the sofa whilst still holding a can of beer. Mrs Hough came into the room at full-time, tutted when she saw her husband asleep and made Jerry and herself a cup of tea. She even stayed with Jerry during extra-time, which proved to be equally tedious – both teams seemed tired and unwilling to take any risks. This merely confirmed Mrs Hough's suspicion regarding football being a waste of time, so she returned to her work before the real drama of a penalty shoot-out began.

The Crawley goalkeeper already stood behind his line watching the Portuguese striker place the ball on the penalty spot, when Jerry decided to wake his dad up.

"Have they started again yet?" came his dad's voice.

"Penalties. You haven't missed a thing." Jerry felt genuinely nervous and could hardly watch.

The first penalty flew in, past Crawley's diving goalie. Jerry shared the frustration with millions of others. Crawley Town's celebrated striker, stepped up, took two steps and casually slid the ball into the right hand corner. Millions sighed with relief.

Then the other Portuguese striker scored easily, which put Crawley under pressure. However, all the next five penalties went in, leaving it 4-4. The opponents' fifth penalty taker was a young Brazilian often described as the next Pele. With a cocky assurance he stood over the ball with no intention of even taking a run-up.

"Miss, you chav," snarled Jerry's dad.

Aware of the scratches on the lenses again and his poor vision, Jerry took his glasses off to give them a wipe on the hem of his shirt. As he did so, a scream from his dad startled him. Fumbling to replace his glasses, he tried to focus on the television when his dad pulled his hand and hugged him tightly.

"Yes! Yes! He's bloody saved it!"

Once released, Jerry peered at the screen where another replay began. The Brazilian nonchalantly chipped the ball completely straight, scuffing it slightly whilst the Crawley keeper kept his nerve, stayed his ground and caught it with two hands before casually rolling it back. The referee managed to stop a big brawl and things calmed down to allow the Crawley captain his big moment. He carefully repositioned the ball, took a dozen steps backwards, then whacked it so hard it nearly burst through the back of the net.

Sharing another hug and a dance with his dad became a moment for Jerry to treasure.

"Yes. Bloody, sodding yes!" Mr Hough screamed.

"I can't believe it," Jerry struggled to swallow back the tears.

"We're only in the sodding Champions sodding League final."

"Awesome."

When Jerry's mum descended to find out the score she nodded with feigned interest and then made the fatal error.

"But it's only a silly game."

Father and son shook their heads pitifully and blanked her for the rest of the evening. Mr Hough went to the fridge for another beer.

Chapter Four

Whilst he was getting changed for PE the next morning, a message reached his teacher to send Jerry to Mr Platt's office immediately. Disappointed to be missing football, Jerry left his clothes and bag hanging up, prodded his wonky glasses up his nose, left the sports hall and strolled towards the appropriate building. Had Platt finally worked out how to protect him from the likes of Wayno? This thought comforted him until he realised he'd never mentioned the identity of the bully to anyone. Perhaps they'd found the CCTV footage of his moment of humiliation and would offer him victim-support and counselling.

Jerry knocked on the office door.

After a long pause he heard the command to enter.

As Jerry walked in he noticed Platt faced the door this time, staring into a laptop which shone onto his lengthy forehead.

"How?" Platt spoke without looking up.

Jerry screwed up his face in confusion. How what? Was this a traditional Native American greeting? If so Jerry didn't know the polite response. Should he light a fire and try some smoke signals?

"Sorry sir?"

"It's how isn't it?"

"How what, sir?"

"Don't get funny with me boy." Platt's tone changed to a snarl.

"I'm not, sir. I don't understand what you mean." Jerry couldn't stand another silly conversation especially as he still only stood in the doorway.

"Are you Jerry How?"

Then came the realisation. Platty couldn't pronounce his surname. Once again the teacher continued to live up to his nickname.

"It's Hough. Jerry Hough." He really wanted to add '007, licensed to kill', but it would have only got him a detention.

"Huff?" Mr Platt questioned with narrowed eyes as if he suspected Jerry of lying about his identity. Jerry wondered if the man even remembered their meeting the day before.

"As in 'I'll huff and I'll puff and I'll blow your house down'," Jerry found himself saying.

"Yes, well, anyway – come in and close the door," Mr Platt looked disconcerted. When Mr Platt nodded towards a chair, Jerry guessed he should sit on it. Sudden movements, he discovered this morning, caused his glasses to slip down at an angle, probably due to the fact they were broken beyond repair.

"Well, um, Jerry," Mr Platt began in his mildest tone. "We have some very interesting CCTV footage from yesterday. I wondered what you have to say for yourself."

This last question seemed a bit strange, but Jerry felt glad the bullying would be over from now on.

"It's been happening for some time now…"

"Has it indeed?" One of Mr Platt's eyebrows arched high and the other frowned as he tapped furiously on the keyboard of his laptop.

"Yes. It began in year 7 and the same people are still involved." Jerry enjoyed the sensation of finally confessing something constantly haunting his dreams and waking hours for so long. It was for the greater good and worth saving others from the same pain and humiliation.

"There are others you say?"

"Yes, of course," Jerry answered, confused.

"I see." Platt's eyebrow rose again and his head nodded as he tap-tap-tapped on his keyboard.

Jerry started to lose confidence in this meeting. Surely it must show clearly on the film the sizeable crowd gathering round him, although it wouldn't surprise him if Mr Platt was scared of Wayno. In fact, Jerry would probably get suspended for doing a moony in the corridor.

"So this has been going on for a long time, you say?" Mr Platt asked with another tap-tap-tap. "How often does it occur?"

"Most days."

"Really?" Mr Platt sounded less than sympathetic. "Then it seems this problem is far worse than we at first suspected. I thought it might just be a one off. But now you are confessing to a whole series of misdemeanours."

Hang on, thought Jerry. 'Misdemeanours'? But I'm the victim here.

"And I'd very much like to hear about these others you say are also involved," Mr Platt added with a growing tone of triumph in his voice.

Jerry adjusted his glasses and when he saw the teacher's look of malevolence he lost his nerve.

"But, sir, I don't understand ..."

"I am going to phone your parents and get them in to discuss this further. This needs to be dealt with now before it becomes a problem for the EWO." Mr Platt scrolled through SIMS and found Jerry's home contact details. "Both parents are at work, I see. I'll try your father's mobile."

Jerry sat back, flummoxed. His sense of normality had been suddenly bent out of shape. Did Wayno have some supernatural power with which he could manipulate the film to make Jerry look like the aggressor?

He watched as Mr Platt pressed a series of buttons on the phone and sat back in his red swivel chair as it rang. Jerry's dad answered quickly.

"Um, hello? Is that Mr How?" the Head of Year began. Jerry

put a hand to his mouth to suppress his laughter. He could make out his dad's voice expressing a certain confusion.

"Um, How … er … oh yes, sorry, I mean Huff. Yes, well … Mr Hough. That's it. Anyway, I have your son here, um …" Mr Platt peered at his laptop screen, having clearly forgotten the name already, "Jerry. Jerry Hough."

Mr Hough's voice sounded impatient and Jerry couldn't wait to see the showdown between Platt and his dad.

"I'm just phoning to inform you that your son has been caught truanting from school. I have him here with me now and it appears there is a bigger problem which we need to discuss with you further."

So that explained it. Jerry closed his eyes and tapped the heel of his hand on his temple. He'd been caught walking out of school and this wasn't about the bullying incident at all. Typical, he thought; they have cameras to check truancy by the front gates but none in the corridors where the real trouble happens. He should know better than to think a school might actually care about its pupils.

Then he thought about the ridiculous conversation with Platt completely at cross purposes. Now Mr Platt thought he bunked every day and he'd said others were involved. How to get out of this one? Jerry considered his plight carefully. With his dad coming in to school it seemed a better idea to wait for him before giving a full confession. Whilst his parents knew nothing about the bullying, it seemed bound to come out now, so telling the truth appeared to be the best policy.

"Yes, thanks, um, Mr Hough. Right. See you soon, then." Mr Platt replaced the phone and sat back with a smug smile. "Wait here Jeremy. Your father will be joining us in about twenty minutes. You understand that truancy can lead to a temporary exclusion. What have you got to say for yourself?"

"My name's not Jeremy."

"I beg your pardon?" Mr Platt stood up and stared at the pupil with a frown.

"It's not Jeremy. My parents called me just Jerry. That's the name on my birth certificate."

Platt's voice rose to a yell as he went red in the face.

"Don't you dare take that tone of voice with me! Who do you think you are? You're in enough trouble already. Your attitude is disgraceful! You now have an after school detention for rudeness! Now sit there in absolute silence! Not a word from you! Do you hear?"

Jerry nodded meekly and sat right back, leaning his head against the pinboard behind him. With a headache beginning he closed his eyes, willing the next twenty minutes to pass quickly.

When a noise stirred him, Jerry realised he must have been dozing. The office door opened and he saw Mr Platt ushering his dad into the room. Jerry automatically stood up.

"Alright, son?" Mr Hough nodded to Jerry. "What's all this about exactly?"

Mr Platt took his place behind his laptop and motioned for the two of them to sit down. "First of all I'll furnish you with the facts and then you will both have a chance to express your views." The Head of Year placed his splayed fingers together like a spider doing press-ups on a mirror.

"Mr How...uff," Platt looked at Jerry's dad wide-eyed, "your son, Jerry, was seen on CCTV cameras leaving school at precisely 2.57pm. We take a very dim view on truancy, which as you know not only breaks school rules but contravenes British Law itself. Jerry was summoned to my office this morning and he has confessed to regular truancy. It sounds like there is a whole group involved and that this problem needs a great deal of investigation. Truancy from school involves the Educational Welfare Officer who works in conjunction with parents and Social Services to make sure attendance issues are adhered to. This is a very serious matter which is generally punishable with a sanction known as a fixed-term exclusion. Now then this may involve either being put in isolation or being suspended ..."

"Yeah, I know what it is thanks – you don't need to patronise me," Mr Hough interrupted, looking annoyed. Jerry wanted to punch the air.

"So taking into account the seriousness of this defiant behaviour, I believe his punishment ..." Mr Platt continued to intone.

"Stop. Just stop talking, Mr ... what's your name again?"

"Um, Platt."

"Well, Mr Umplatt." (Jerry marvelled at his dad's nerve, but enjoyed watching Platt begin to squirm). "If you've quite finished maybe I can get a word in edgeways. You see I just don't buy it. I think I know my son a little better than you do and I know for a fact my son is not someone who bunks off school without good reason. He's doing very well in his studies and to my knowledge has never been in major trouble before. But now you suddenly tell me he might be suspended. You claim he's persistently truanting but I'm pretty confident that if there was a problem he'd have told us about it. The other thing that occurs to me, which doesn't seem to have occurred to you, is that if he is, as you say, allegedly skipping school, which I doubt, then maybe there's a reason for it. Have you actually listened to Jerry's point of view yet? Shall we see what Jerry has to say about it?"

Jerry wanted to hug his dad. The Head of Year nodded meekly, shuffling and mumbling inaudibly.

"So then Jerry," his dad said, having now taken over this meeting, "the floor's yours. What the hell is really going on here?"

Jerry sat up properly and tried to find the right words.

"I did leave school yesterday at about three ..."

"There, you see ..." began Mr Platt, quickly silenced by the raising of a finger and a stern expression which Jerry knew well.

29

"But that's the first time I've ever skived. You see yesterday I got bullied ... again." He looked up quickly to gauge his dad's reaction; Mr Hough's eyes narrowed but both adults were intently listening. "I've been bullied for quite a few years now and I've managed to cope okay with it to a point but yesterday got pretty bad. I'm teased for wearing glasses mostly, called 'four eyes' and all the rest of it, but yesterday got a bit more violent than usual. I was punched, my glasses got broken," Jerry took them off as if passing an item of evidence around court, "and then they debagged me in the corridor."

"Debagged?" Mr Platt queried.

"Oh, for God's sake, man. Pulled his trousers down." Jerry's dad sounded exasperated. "Didn't they do that in your day?"

Jerry wondered if Mr Platt himself had been bullied at school. It wouldn't surprise him.

"So this bullying incident happened yesterday?" Mr Platt bravely tried to get some control back. "Why didn't you report it?" The smirk on lips gave him a high and mighty air, until he heard Jerry's quick reply.

"I did."

"Oh. Who to?"

"You, sir."

Mr Platt began tapping on his laptop. "But I have no record of this incident."

"Are you calling my son a liar?" Mr Hough blurted.

"No, it's okay dad." He gestured for his dad to stop. "You have no record because you sent me to Mr Finn. So I did and he listened but then told me I should go back to you. I thought you wouldn't listen and tell me off again, so I panicked and admit I was stupid to leave school. I don't mind doing a punishment for that because I broke the rules and hold my hands up. But I also went because I was scared of having to explain it all to the teacher. I really thought the best use of my time would be to go home and catch up on all my homework. I promise I went straight home and did all my work. I'm totally up to date now with everything."

Jerry looked at his dad who was smiling proudly at him.

"So you didn't listen to my son when he came to report that he'd been bullied?" Mr Hough leaned in towards the cowering Mr Platt. "What's going on here? It's a bloody disgrace. What kind of school is this? I thought it was your job to protect children."

"Mr Finn said he'd email you. Perhaps you haven't read the email yet?" Jerry said the words innocently, knowing he could only say these things because of his dad's presence.

"Haven't really had a chance yet ..." Mr Platt mumbled, nervously looking at his laptop screen and pushing a few buttons.

"Well?" Jerry's dad sounded more like the strict teacher in this scenario with Platt now the naughty little boy.

"Um, there does seem to be something, yes," Mr Platt's eyes quickly scanned the screen. "Well, I apologise for wasting your time and ..."

"You haven't wasted my time, Mr Umplatt. We've discovered that my son is being bullied in your school and it seems it's your job to do something about it. I would like some kind of reassurance that you will catch the perpetrators, stop this nonsense and support Jerry by ensuring this never happens again. If you don't then I will certainly take this further by going to the council, press or my local MP."

"I should like to reassure you that we have a zero-tolerance view of bullying in this school and every step will be taken to stop this incident from escalating." Mr Platt said the line like a sales pitch.

"Glad to hear it," Jerry's dad replied. "You're lucky I'm not contacting the police about this. Those kids who punched my son should be in prison..."

"We don't need the police, Mr Hough. Please rest assured this will be dealt with in the proper manner."

"Right now?"

31

"Yes, right now. Jerry can tell me all the details and give me names and I'll make a full report and take it from there," Mr Platt reached out for some different coloured forms.

"And when he's finished he's going to have the rest of the day off," Mr Hough stated unequivocally. "He needs time to recuperate from his injury and trauma." He turned and winked to his son. "Plus I am going to take him to the opticians this afternoon to get him some new glasses. Okay, Jerry? When you've finished here you go straight home. I need to sort a few things out at work then I'll be home for lunch and we'll go into town." He turned to Mr Platt. "Do I need to write a note to authorise today's absence or do you think you might be able to manage that one on your own?"

"No, no. I'll phone the school office and sort it out," Mr Platt mumbled, blinking in one eye as Mr Hough stood up to go.

"Good-o." He turned to his son. "See you later, mate." Mr Hough squeezed Jerry's shoulder and left without saying goodbye to the teacher. This weird meeting certainly helped Jerry to see his own dad in quite a new light. He turned to Mr Platt now with a fresh confidence.

Chapter Five

Jerry's dad stuck to his word. He arrived home just over an hour later; made them both lunch, then took Jerry in to town. At the opticians Jerry only had to wait about five minutes before being called to the back of the shop for his eye test.

A smiling middle-aged lady read his name from a file and ushered him into a little booth full of equipment and charts. Jerry always had problems pronouncing the word ophthalmologist.

"Hello, Jerry. How are you, today?"

"Fine thanks," Jerry answered with a nervous look. He took off his coat and sat down on the chair which she motioned him towards.

"Just try and relax, Jerry. It's called a test but it's not like being at school – we're not trying to catch you out or anything. I'm going to ask you a few questions and you just need to answer them as honestly as you can."

Jerry nodded meekly. He felt like a prisoner of war about to be tortured. Luckily the smiling lady seemed kind and gentle, but this might be a ruse to soften him up before turning nasty.

"Your records show you were born with a squint, is that right?"

"Yes and I had some operations when I was about two, I think."

"Uhuh, to correct them. And which eye would you say is the stronger of the two?"

"Um, my left eye can see further than my right."

"And has that always been the case?"

"No, I'm sure my right eye used to be stronger, but now it's changed." Jerry was glad to tell someone about this phenomenon and he felt like some kind of weirdo. It came as quite a relief when the lady merely smiled as if this seemed perfectly normal.

"So would you say one of your eyes is dominant?"

"Yes, my right eye is the one I'm most aware of looking out of. Sometimes people say my left eye goes all funny or looks in the wrong direction." Once again Jerry cringed, expecting her to press a button and call for him to be taken away to the Circus of Freaks.

"Uhuh, a lazy eye. Perfectly common." Then the lady reeled off a couple of long scientific sounding terms which meant nothing to him. She scribbled more notes and then looked at him again with a very broad smile.

"I see from your notes that contact lenses aren't really an option to you."

Jerry nodded. He always had to explain things and he knew the right words to use.

"Yes, I tried them before and they reacted badly with my cornea and the doctor warned me about keratitis."

She looked again at the notes, humming in agreement.

"Yes, yes, sensitive cornea and conjunctiva. The lenses can irritate your lachrymal glands..."

"Which makes me look like a cry-baby," Jerry said. "Not good for the street cred."

"And why are you getting new glasses today?"

"These ones got broken," he explained taking them off gingerly. "Er, when I was playing football."

"Do you mind?" she asked, holding out her hand to take them from him. "Goodness, they are damaged aren't they?" Jerry nodded. "Well, we have got some good deals on at the moment so we'll see what discounts we can do for you. And it's a good idea to get a spare pair in case this happens again – we're doing a two for one deal at the moment."

Jerry waited for the ophthalmologist to jot down a few more notes before she put down his glasses and looked up again.

"Right then, Jerry. You've done all this before so you don't need to worry. It's all quite straight forward."

Then came the instruments of torture. The test began with fine powder being blown into his eyes before bright lights blinded him.

"Just checking for cataracts."

He assumed there were none as nothing else was said.

Then he had to look through a machine and try to match up two lines in a series of tests, which he knew meant his eyes did not work together. He could never see certain optical illusions like those 'stereograms' because his eyes only worked independently of each other. He also remembered having a bit of trouble with 3D films when the two images didn't quite match up and usually gave him a headache. He felt as if he was missing out on something really fun – as if he might be the only one who couldn't see what everyone else could.

Then when he looked through the contraption at the letters and numbers he felt a wonderful sense of relief when a lens dropped in front of his eye. Suddenly everything appeared brighter and stronger. It was the miracle of technology and a wonderful feeling of liberation when he could focus on that bottom row of letters.

Eventually they were both happy with the choice of lenses and Jerry was allowed to go back to his dad. The smiling lady walked with him and entered into a short conversation with Mr Hough.

"Yes, he's fine. His eyesight has got a little worse – only fractionally. It's what we'd expect with someone born with a squint; nothing to worry about. Jerry has a classic case of myopia."

Jerry liked the sound of that word: myopia. It sounded like an exotic island – not a million miles away from utopia. He'd heard about Utopia in English lessons: the perfect place according to some dead bloke called Thomas More. Well, he thought myopia sounded even lovelier. The name had a pleasant ring to it – a delicious word to roll around your mouth. It had shape and curves and a lilting sensuality about it. Such treasures, adventures and thrilling dangers waited to be found there. Here in Myopia, all your dreams come true.

The spell was quickly broken when Jerry realised his dad was trying on all the spectacles in the shop including all the ones for ladies.

"Dad, put them back and help me look for mine."

Jerry settled on a trendy, neat pair that his dad swore made him look sophisticated.

"Loads of cool people wore glasses: John Lennon, Michael Caine, Johnny Depp, Superman … um … yeah loads of them." He dismissed the fact with a wave of the hand as though he deemed the point so obvious it didn't really need justification.

Jerry remained unconvinced although he could name quite a few A-list celebrities who wore glasses as fashion accessories. Some sports stars wore glasses, even when running or playing, such as Dutch footballer Edgar Davids. In some sports such as sprinting or cricket, wearing shades had almost become the norm. Jerry knew this was cheating slightly as sunglasses were acceptably cool, whilst spectacles in films usually indicated the wearer to be an egghead, librarian, loner or pensioner. Quite often the glasses became a prop to cover up the wearer's glamour, finally revealed when the specs got thrown away.

At the counter, the bored girl who only looked a few years older than Jerry, reminded them about the 'two for one' offer.

"You can select another pair from these frames at the end of the counter."

Of course the choice was horribly limited to classic NHS horn-rimmed and revolting two-tones with tortoiseshell effect. Eventually Jerry settled for a pair of small round frames that he could certainly use should he ever choose to go to a fancy dress party as Harry Potter.

It always came as a shock when he heard the price; even though he still counted as a child the charge seemed astronomical. He'd better start saving up now to afford glasses as an adult. His dad reached for his wallet and with thumb and forefinger fished out his credit card. But before he could hand it over to the bored girl she suddenly piped up with her extra sales pitch.

"Can I interest you in our non-scratch lens coating? It's added during the process and guarantees against scratches and damage to the lens surface."

Mr Hough looked to Jerry who shrugged.

"Go on then. It might save them next time he plays football."

"We can also add light sensitive tinting; non-glare solar protection; a light-increasing treatment for when it gets darker."

Both Jerry and his dad shook their heads with mouths twisted in a slight sneer.

"I can offer you our new cleaning spray and cloth which is soft non-scratch material..." the girl continued, undeterred.

"No. No thanks – just the glasses will be fine." Mr Hough sounded impatient.

The girl looked slightly confused from being interrupted in the middle of her well-rehearsed spiel. After flicking her eyes from side to side a few times, she picked it up again; still with a look of extreme boredom on her face.

"Then you'll be wanting our protection cover in case of damge, breakages, theft, loss, fire and even scratches..."

"But we've just asked for non-scratch lenses, I'm not paying more for the same guarantee," Mr Hough cried out with a pained expression.

This threw the girl completely who obviously had not been trained up for this eventuality.

"And theft? Why would anybody steal somebody's

prescription glasses?"

The girl behind the counter looked more baffled than bored now.

His dad carried on his rant. "Look I don't want to buy anything else or spend any more money. These glasses are bloody expensive and you're still trying to scrounge even more out of me."

Gingerly she took Mr Hough's card and pressed a number of keys on her till, which eventually displayed the final total. The non-scratch coating cost almost half the price again making Jerry feel guilty.

Once the transaction was complete the girl, whose face had returned to its 'look of boredom' setting, let them have the bad news.

"You can pick those up after eleven o'clock tomorrow."

"But I thought we only had to wait an hour? That's what it says in your window and on your advert on telly." Jerry's dad began to sound ruffled.

"Not if you order the non-scratch coating…"

"Well, you could have bloody well told us…"

"Come on, Dad, let's go." Jerry pulled his dad's arm and eventually Mr Hough gave in, growling at the now startled girl. "It's fine," Jerry added. "It doesn't matter."

"No, it does matter," Mr Hough replied fervently. "My son needs these specs to see properly. You claim to be offering a service to help people with bad eyesight, but you're just in it for a quick profit. Money-grabbing capitalists!"

Jerry hauled him away rapidly and pushed him in the direction of the car park, away from the many staring eyes of other shoppers and passers-by.

Chapter Six

After seeing things so clearly through the opticians' lenses it became relatively obvious just how damaged his old glasses were. Even with his 'Speckless Specs' cleaning spray and the scientifically-tested, non-abrasive 'Softy-cloth', they were impossible to clean properly. Grime somehow lodged itself into the tiny cracks and whilst the starburst effects looked pretty in the evening when he peered at colourful lights and swung his head about, he realised how these glasses were not doing their job any more. Seeing glimpses of things out the corner of his eye and around the edges of them started to make him slightly paranoid when he kept turning at every movement in his peripheral vision.

Without his glasses the world looked rather strange. Seeing two of each item before him reminded him of his squint. His baby photos always made people either hoot with laughter or coo in sympathy. The one of him lying in his cot showed baby Jerry gazing upwards with his left eye looking across to his own nose, and the right pupil rolling upwards practically looking behind him. His dad used to guffaw loudly and call him 'My little chameleon', which Jerry only understood later when he saw a TV documentary on weird creatures celebrating the independent eye movements of these fascinating reptiles. Jerry kind of saw the joke and often considered teaching as a career; what with eyes practically in the back of his head.

Then the photos showed him growing into a schoolboy with blue round glasses and then classic NHS Woody Allen glasses. The family album included the compulsory 'patch over one eye' shot and Jerry remembered those sticky patches he'd had to put over one lens – certain he also recalled having to shove cotton wool over one eye, kept in place by a pirate's patch with elastic round his head. It explained why his grandpa had called him 'Jim-lad' for so long, although he still didn't know what 'pieces of eight' were.

The one photo his mum chose to enlarge, frame and hang up in the front room showed him wearing a bobble hat, duffel coat and red wellies. With his little brown glasses under the woolly hat it always looked to Jerry like the face of a garden gnome grinning back out into the world. He never associated himself with the strange little creature in that picture and he even made up stories and gave the silly character a name: Gnobby the Gnome.

Now his world was misted up: without glasses it fuzzed into its usual myopic frenzy. (Jerry had been excited to find his own adjective to describe his blurry world), and with these broken glasses it was foggy and distracting. How wonderful his new pair seemed already. Once obtained, he would have a new view on the world and his mum promised to pick him up tomorrow lunchtime to go and get them. He had one murky night and hazy morning to get through before clarity returned and became once more rightfully his.

As he sat in bed reading, Jerry put down his book and slipped off his glasses which were beginning to annoy him. He pinched the corners of his eyes with thumb and forefinger, aware of the distant signs of an in-coming headache. Then came the usual contemplation: could he be bothered to go and get some tablets?

He found himself in a weird situation - his body and eyes felt incredibly tired and achy (they screamed out for rest and unconsciousness – the chance to stop working and lie dormant as the energy slowly seeped back into them, hoping to awake tomorrow refreshed and full of newfound vigour and zest) but his mind buzzed with thoughts and memories. His stupid brain felt horribly active, revisiting events and feelings experienced over the last few days. Jerry knew sleep should be his priority and turned over for at least the hundredth time to try again. But how can you sleep when images and words and emotions and regrets and fears and unfulfilled wishes and feelings of embarrassment and intimidation and confusion and doubt and a sense of worthlessness all clamour and crowd your horribly wakeful mind?

Wayno and Rhino dominated his thoughts as he recalled for the zillionth time how they'd made him flash his private parts in public. What goes through a person's head to think it's okay to make another human being feel so worthless and humiliated? It seemed to Jerry to be the lowest act a human could descend to.

Then Jerry considered the teachers. Quincy at least offered him some sanctuary of peace and hope, which in the scheme of things showed him to be a kind man with good intentions. But Platt, it seemed to Jerry, might as well be on the side of the bullies. The only thing to cheer him up slightly was the memory of his dad making Platt live up to his nick-name.

What of Miss Powys? Jerry knew a secret he desperately wanted to tell Silu, his best friend, but couldn't. He realised she must be going through hell at the moment and began to think of ways he could be nice to her.

Without warning, Mindy came into his head. There she stood with her dimpled smile gazing at him intently through those hazel brown eyes. With Mindy in his head the horror passed. He turned over and felt himself slipping happily towards sleep as if he rolled gently down a slight hill into the soft warmth of eternal relaxation … smothered … covered in gentleness and a caressing, soothing embrace.

Then he felt himself fall and woke up. Coming to with a start Jerry realised he had experienced that stupid night time thing of dreaming he'd fallen off a cliff, but the falling motion had woken him. Urban legend has it that if you continue falling without waking up – you die. Jerry couldn't help feeling grateful. Looking at his alarm clock he saw the time was 4:27. Damn! He'd been hoping it was closer to seven and time to get up. And he still had a thumping headache.

Fluffing up his pillows and pushing them against the headboard of his bed, Jerry sat up without putting on either the light or his glasses. Even though his curtains were lined it didn't seem very dark in his bedroom. Whilst all the familiar objects and posters were blurred, he could still make out their shapes and identify them easily in the half-light. It always amazed him how eyes could get used to darkness.

Jerry felt an unexpected urge to get up and see if he could get downstairs without being heard by his mum who had the preternatural hearing of a cat. Before leaving his warm, cosy bed to test the cold air, Jerry remained seated for a few more minutes. Looking about him he closed one eye and then the other. This had the weird effect of shifting objects slightly to one side and then back again as if it kept flicking left then right. It also dimmed things slightly. He noticed how objects, even in the gloaming, appeared a bit brighter through his right eye and duller through his left, and he wondered why it should be so.

When something moved in his peripheral vision he turned his head slowly in that direction. He had grown used to such happenings as glasses often caught reflections on lenses and on shiny frames, so such events didn't faze him. But then it occurred to him he wasn't wearing glasses at the moment. This seemed a new phenomenon. Perhaps something had moved in his room. Was it the curtain? A car light? His fevered imagination? Probably nothing – just something in his eye. It reminded Jerry of those strange lights and falling stars you can see sometimes when you close your eyes, as if your eyelids have their own firework display.

Looking around his room he could see nothing out of the ordinary. There was a faint glow around his door from the night light in the landing; he made out his Crawley FC posters, the clock, his bookcase and his chair, draped in yesterday's clothes. Then craning his ear in the direction of the door he listened intently without breathing for half a minute, but the only sound he heard was his Dad snoring – and it occurred to Jerry how much it really did sound like someone sawing logs.

If he swivelled his head right round to the left he could see his curtains. This always seemed like the most vulnerable part of the room – more so than the door. A door is solid, opaque, lockable, whilst a window is transparent and fragile. Jerry would happily open and walk through a door in the middle of the night, but if asked to push back a curtain and look out into the darkness he would consider it with some trepidation. Imagine the horror of peeking behind your curtain and out of your own bedroom window only to be confronted by a white, glaring, malevolent face.

When he saw a movement at the curtain he wondered if he'd left a window open which would have allowed a breeze to cause it to flutter. But no window was open – it would've felt a lot colder otherwise. So the movement could not be explained by the wind. Without his glasses he could just make out the stripes created by the hanging pleats alternately dark and light which accentuated its length. As he stared it appeared to billow and then, even more weirdly, to detach itself and float slowly towards him. Not his curtains exactly – Jerry remained aware that his curtains had stayed where they were, but a semblance of his curtains seemed to be hanging very closely before him as well. At first he thought it might be a ghost but that didn't seem right somehow. Whilst he'd never seen a ghost before he'd always imagined they would be vengeful and scary. This didn't offer him any immediate threat but just floated there in a neutral way, billowing slightly. As he watched on it got slowly smaller like an ebbing ocean and returned to the curtains. Jerry thought he may have just witnessed a fantastic

43

phenomenon, but on the other hand he had got used to seeing strange things without his glasses and felt convinced it could be explained by his myopia, which frequently played funny tricks on him.

Jerry knew he should just grab his glasses to clear up the mystery, but if he was honest he enjoyed the mystery more than the dull reality an answer would provide.

Then he heard an unexpected noise from downstairs. It wasn't his parents as he could faintly hear them both snoring in harmony. Jerry considered waking them, but thought it cowardly. Being out of bed meant he felt obliged to go downstairs to investigate. It would prove to be nothing he felt sure, but he wanted to go and look just to make certain; and whilst there get some headache tablets and a glass of water.

The stairs lay before him as his first obstacle. Steps numbers three and eight (coming down) he knew to avoid, especially at night with his mum's super-powered hearing. Jerry gripped the banister tightly and with a stretch nearly as wide as the splits his foot reached step four. Then with his weight on the rail he shifted his other foot down until both stood firmly on the solid and silent step. Creeping down he successfully reached the bottom even after nearly tripping over a coat he remembered abandoning earlier on the bottom step.

Once downstairs he breathed a sigh of relief and stood motionless in the hallway for a few moments. Then he remembered the sound from earlier. Although scared at the prospect of meeting a stranger in his house, the thought excited him – he felt the adrenaline pumping through him. Fear was something to be enjoyed and relished.

Jerry opened the door of the sitting room with a glacial slowness. A vaguely orange glow from the lamppost outside their house shone through a gap in the curtains and he could just make out the familiar objects such as the sofa, television and coffee table. However he wasn't expecting there to be a shape under the coffee table that he swore might be a crouching figure - curled up with head tucked in hands as if playing hide and seek. He inched closer, knelt down next to it and reached out with his right hand to gently place it on the back of the person he'd convinced himself was there. Jerry even felt its warmth and the rise and fall of its breathing. Gripping hold and tugging it he even witnessed it unfold its limbs and lift its head. But when the head unexpectedly fell off and the arms swung emptily, Jerry could clearly see that it was his mum's woollen hooded cardigan which had been rolled up and tidied away. It had been an effective illusion.

Because his house was open-plan Jerry could get from the sitting room into the kitchen, which itself led to the utility room and back round to the stairs again. As a child he had often enjoyed chasing his dad round and round the house in circles of fun during those never ending summer holidays. In the kitchen the first thing he spotted made him start, but with pleasure rather than fear. There next to the sink he recognised his old friend the unicorn, its unmistakable shape neatly silhouetted against the security lights from the house whose garden adjoined theirs. How he wished the unicorn might step down for him to climb upon its back and to ride far away to a land of adventure and chivalry. To the mystical world of Myopia where Jerry could be a hero instead of a four-eyed saddo who was regularly bullied. In Myopia he was a warrior, a secret agent, a gigolo, a rock star. The more he stared and allowed his eyes to go out of focus, the clearer he could see. Suddenly the unicorn lifted its head shaking a lengthy mane. Then it gracefully rose before him and trotted forwards obediently and he could swear he heard its hooves echo on the tiled flooring. Shaking his head with a jerk, Jerry then made the vision disappear.

There seemed to be no sign of an intruder or a break-in, which relieved him greatly. In the kitchen he opened the cupboard containing the medicine box and found what he hoped were the paracetamol rather than the laxatives which were packaged in a similar white box. Jerry swallowed two tablets with a swig of lemonade from the bottle he knew would be on the main work surface. Whilst his temples and eyeballs continued to pulsate he placed his thumbs carefully over his closed eyelids and gently massaged the soft roundness beneath.

Walking through the utility room with its cold linoleum flooring, Jerry reached the hallway and stood at the bottom of the stairs. In absolute silence he stood statically for what seemed like an interminably long time. Was it hours or minutes? He dared not move or make a noise as he felt convinced he might hear that sound again – any second now. When his stomach made a whining noise he tensed up. Then he tried opening and closing his mouth to see how silently he could breath. Outside the faint hum of traffic came and went. Eventually Jerry began to realise how cold he was. The central heating didn't come on until about 6am, and he had no dressing gown or socks on. Suddenly the warm cosy allure of his bed became too much for him; except he couldn't move. With all the waiting and listening it was as if his body had moulded into this statuesque pose and he required a surge of effort in his mind to break the spell. It became a battle: which would break first – his physical or mental will?

Then a movement in the sitting room distracted him as his mind conjured up pictures of intruders ready to threaten him and his family. Perhaps when they heard him come downstairs they had hidden and were now biding their time – he remembered reading about such things. Jerry felt his skin ripple into gooseflesh.

From where he stood he could just see through the sitting-room doorway and morbid curiosity made him turn his head to look. How he wished he had his glasses. He saw definite movements through the misty haze. A figure began to unroll itself from beneath the coffee table.

Jerry stepped quickly backwards and fled upstairs, two at a

time.

"Mum! Dad!"

Jerry's mum was the first in to see her son trembling in the landing.

"Oh, my poor darling. What's wrong? You don't look at all well."

"What's all the shouting?" Jerry's dad stumbled in, still half asleep.

"I think Jerry's ill. He's been sleep-walking or something, poor love."

Seeing his parents made Jerry feel much better. He almost forgot about the terrifying experiences, but then remembered about the intruders.

"There's someone downstairs. I saw something."

"Really?" Jerry's dad turned immediately. "We'll see about that."

Jerry listened to his dad descend the stairs and walk round the house. He could hear his slippers on the kitchen and utility room floor. When he heard his dad fill the kettle and return upstairs he guessed there was no sign of any intruders.

"All clear downstairs. No one there and nothing missing. You had a nightmare, mate." He turned to his wife who was still comforting Jerry. "Remember he used to have night terrors when he was younger."

Jerry felt insulted. "Yeah, when I was four."

"Everyone has nightmares," said his mum soothingly. "You go back to bed, love."

Jerry's dad tutted and disappeared into the toilet where he would remain for the next twenty minutes.

Chapter Seven

Jerry enjoyed the next day at home. His mum refused to let him go to school with such a temperature and she'd convinced his dad to let him have a day off. Mrs Hough collected his new glasses on the condition that he stayed in bed, which wasn't a very difficult choice.

Holding the new case in his hands with great reverence he prised it open with both thumbs, like opening an oyster in search of a pearl. There it lay, the shining treasure. He pinched the wire arms delicately between thumb and forefinger and lifted them slowly, whilst snapping shut the case with his other hand. He'd forgotten what they looked like and it surprised him how much lighter and smaller they were than his previous pair. Having removed his old ones Jerry carefully opened the wire arms with their tiny hinges until the rounded ends of the frames that went over his ears were pointing towards his eyes. Then with delicate precision he slid the ends under his hair and round the tops of his ears; as he did so the lenses loomed and then rose over his nose and slipped into position.

What bliss. Such clarity. It was as if he had reached spiritual enlightenment. He suddenly understood the meaning of life. Going from fuzzy madness to focussed reality also returned his sense of reason. These new glasses offered him a vista full of colours where every line was straight, objects looked sharp and finally made sense. There were no misty patches or scratches which distracted him continually. Here was a sensible, logical world. No visions, shadows or moving forms lived here. Proudly wearing his new glasses made him wonder if the world of Myopia was quite all he had imagined it to be.

With new vision Jerry clambered out of bed and ambled to the bathroom to look at himself in the cabinet mirror. These were much smaller than his last pair and only just seemed to cover his eyes, revealing more of his cheeks and forehead. Yet his reaction was far from a negative one: in fact he felt he preferred them already. Wearing new glasses changed your whole face and usually took some getting used to. He was bound to receive comments tomorrow once back at school but he'd have to ride the blast and smile at each reaction until everyone got bored and his new glasses got forgotten. Such was life.

Back in his room he looked out of the window at the branches of the large oak tree that practically touched the house. His dad had been promising for over a year now to bring his gang round to prune the tree which now loomed dangerously close to their roof and guttering. Jerry's mum despaired that her husband seemed willing to sort out any other tree in West Sussex except their own. As Jerry stared out towards the surrounding houses and gardens he became aware of the frames in his peripheral vision, but guessed he'd get used to it and soon forget they were there.

His day at home proved wonderful and quiet. He completed the novel he'd been reading; began his dad's newspaper crossword, but got stuck after filling in seven words; texted Silu during double Maths to try and get him into trouble, but to Jerry's surprise he received a rude message back almost immediately (a black mark for the teacher); went for a bike ride to test the powers of the new specs (they passed with distinction); ate a whole packet of cream crackers, each one spread liberally with peanut butter; got his dad's climbing ropes out and made a make-shift rope swing from the giant oak's lowest limb; slept for a few hours in a deliciously rare afternoon siesta; then watched one of his dad's horror DVDs.

He felt a bit depressed about having to go back to school tomorrow.

Ironically, it turned out Wayno had been suspended for the rest of the week and so he felt he'd picked the wrong day to pull a sickie. At least there would be some Wayno-free days, although Jerry didn't relish the thought of his return on Monday, especially being the main person who 'dobbed' him in.

Over on the tarmac he saw Silu and a few others playing footie. It looked like four-a-side with rush goalie. Hailing them as he placed his bag with the others, he felt slightly annoyed when no one acknowledged him, but then again he could see that Xan was about to score having nimbly leapt over Silu's sliding tackle. The ball sped towards the empty goal, hit a bag and went in – or at least bounced against the wall in the space representing the goal.

"That was way offside," shouted Silu, annoyed at having been beaten in defence.

"Hiya mate," called Jerry, taking off his blazer and flinging it in the vague direction of his bag. "Looks like you could do with some help here."

"Oh, hi, Jez. Look sorry but we've got equal teams. Wouldn't be fair. Know what I mean?"

"I could be goalie?"

"Nah, can't change things now - this is the World Cup Final. Maybe next time, yeah?" Silu picked up the ball ready to roll it out.

"You could find someone else so we're five aside," offered Matty helpfully. "What you reckon?"

It was Silu's ball so he had the casting vote. He rolled it to Matty who took off on one of his surging runs on the left wing.

"Have you had a haircut?"

"No," smiled Jerry. "Try again."

"Facelift?"

"Ha, ha. No, but you could do with one, you freak." Jerry had missed the cut and thrust of life as a school pupil. "New glasses, mate."

As Silu looked again he didn't notice the opposition looming in a counter attack after Matty had been too easily dispossessed. He heard someone screaming his name, but it was too late as the ball shrieked past his shoulder and crashed into the wall right on the corner of the painted goalposts. Silu swore and there ensued an argument about whether it counted as a goal.

Jerry sighed realising he remained surplus to requirement.

The best part of the day occurred later as he sat alone in the packed lunch room.

"Looking cool, Jerry."

Jerry looked up delighted to see Mindy standing over him flanked between two friends both also with long straight hair, but blonde and brunette unlike Mindy's shiny jet black tresses.

"They're pretty stylish. They suit you," Mindy continued, indicating his glasses. "Like the ones gorgeous Zach Idaho wears in 'Tall, Dark and Handsome'. God, he's lush."

Jerry knew this was high praise indeed.

"Thanks. It takes a while to get used to them."

"You could try contact lenses," one of Mindy's friends suggested.

"But then he wouldn't have the cute glasses," Mindy said as a reprimand.

Jerry screwed up his face. "Nah. I'm not very good with touching my eyeballs. I have trouble putting eyedrops in let alone sticking my fingers in my eye." He paused, in the hope he didn't sound too wimpy. Then he decided that as always honest was the best policy. "I've actually been told my eyes react badly to contact lenses. I have to avoid pressure on the cornea as it affects facial nerves and glands. Apparently wearing them could lead to something called keratitus, so I'll have to stick with the ol' shades, you know. It's not really very tough and cool to wear specs."

"I think you look just fine," Mindy said with a smile that showed her wondrous dimples. "Good for you. Just be yourself, I say."

Her comments had the effect of doubling his courage.

"Well, maybe we could chat more sometime. We could hang out or go somewhere." He wondered if it was really him speaking.

"Yeah, I'd like that." She got up and pushed the chair back in. "Hey, I just wanted to say that you dealt with those idiots really well the other day. I thought you were pretty brave." She gave him a long, steady look and then turned away. "See you later then." She unexpectedly put a warm hand on his shoulder which made his whole being tingle. Before she could go he placed his hand tenderly on hers. He gazed at the smooth brown skin and the exotic, faint patterns of henna on her wrist.

"Sure. Later."

As he watched her leave Jerry tried to remember any part of the conversation he'd just had, but his mind remained completely blank.

Looking at his own reflection wearing the new glasses for ten minutes didn't help as to his eyes he clearly looked nothing like Zach Idaho, so beloved by Mindy. In fact he looked more like one of those goons from the silent comedies: the archetypal victim or clown who is constantly kicked in the backside by the brutish villain. As far as Jerry was concerned he might as well carry a neon sign saying 'I'm a geek please kick my head in'.

In the end Friday was bearable – just. Silu and Matty gave him a bit of sympathy but he didn't see Mindy. He got a few comments and a sharp punch from Rhino when he passed him in the corridor.

In Science they watched an uninspiring film about

photosynthesis and in the darkness he took off his glasses to rub his sore eyes. Jerry welcomed the blurred haze around him – felt a desire to be enveloped by it as if embraced by a loved one. The fact that he could no longer see the film, the other pupils or even much of the classroom lab made him feel happy and content. This was his own place; a world he could escape to where nobody else existed. Around him lay an undiscovered country to explore. This new space or dimension was a private island just for him together with his thoughts and feelings. Gazing about him, Jerry watched the strange flickering of lights that must be the film, but he could no longer hear the droning of the narrator except as a faint hum in the background.

Jerry became aware of some familiar shapes and movements about him. But this time he didn't feel in the least bit scared. To his right a discernible blob of darkness was billowing like a sheet or cloud, but which somehow no longer felt threatening. Then as his mind continued to wander he felt a ripple beneath him that forced him to suddenly grab his desk. Luckily nobody seemed to notice.

The stool he sat on became unexpectedly soft and then began to undulate making him rock to and fro. Looking around he worried that the others would see him and laugh but they were all too absorbed in the film or in their own dreams or whispering to their neighbour. Nobody seemed to see his strange movements. Nobody was even aware of him. Then without warning his stool began to pull away from the work bench until there was such a distance between them that he was no longer part of the class. In fact the wall of the room appeared to have stretched beyond all limits until the science lesson seemed so remote that he no longer felt himself part of it any more. Nobody seemed to be missing him. He could just see the teacher looking round to check her pupils were watching and she seemed content that nothing was amiss. That was when it occurred to him that he could see into the distance without his glasses; a new experience for Jerry. Had his eyesight righted itself?

Jerry knew something odd was going on. Perhaps he found himself in the middle of a waking dream; a reverie of sorts. Yet he felt perfectly self-aware and more alert and awake than usual. Invigorated: that was the word. No, something else was happening to him. Something, or someone, seemed to be messing about with his sense of reality.

When the stool bucked, almost throwing him from its soft warm seat, Jerry looked down to inspect it. What he saw startled him beyond belief. The thin metal legs of the stool had transformed into black, long legs; muscular at the top and tapering into silver hooves. Without warning two of the legs reared up causing Jerry to grab on to his stool. But what had been a wooden seat under his legs and backside now felt soft and leathery. He managed to balance well as if it had always been the most natural thing in the world to him. He seemed to know how to counter-balance and when to shift his weight to and fro so as to stay perfectly balanced whatever happened beneath him. He leaned forward to stroke the mane and long, spiralling horn of his black unicorn.

Jerry laughed. He dug his spurs into the flanks of his trusty mount.

"I am the knight of Myopia. Beware of me, mine enemies. Look into my eyes and know ye fear."

Then he galloped off for a million miles beyond stars and galaxies, through pasts and futures as if he never cared to return ...

...Except he did. With a bump.

At first Jerry thought he was being regaled with cheers and whoops of admiration. But he quickly realised they were taunts and jeers and that he lay prone on the floor, having fallen off his stool. The film still ran and the teacher jumped up to help him to his feet.

"Serves you right, Jerry. I keep telling you lot not to lean back on your chair and that's exactly why I do so, but you never listen. Perhaps this'll make you sit properly in the future. Now let's be quiet and watch the rest of this film or else the whole class will be in detention."

The looks on everyone's faces made him feel stupid and alienated. Even Silu looked at him with disdain.

Jerry felt his face burn with embarrassment and knew his eyesight had returned to short-sightedness as everything became a giant smeary blur.

Chapter Eight

As soon as Jerry woke up on Monday morning he remembered Wayno would be back. It began a horrible heaviness in his gut – that negative feeling which stays with you all day, nagging, reminding you and never allowing you to be completely happy or at ease … with anything.

And sure enough, as Jerry sauntered round the corner towards school there at the front gate stood Wayno, Rhino and several cronies.

"Look he's coming!" one of them called.

"Nah, that's just the way he's walking," another quipped. They all laughed as everyone hanging round or near the gate looked towards Jerry.

Jerry blushed and continued towards them.

"He's got new specs – ain't they gorgeous?" Wayno jeered as he leant against the tall, green, metal post. "That's your disguise right? Like Superman, he wears glasses by day, then when he takes them off he turns into Supergeek."

"Supernerd," snarled Rhino.

"Superfreak," came another voice beginning a long list of swear words attached to the prefix 'super'.

"Not forgetting of course supergrass," Wayno added with a snort. "Thanks for the extra days off school. Saves having to skive." The ring of lads chuckled like eight year olds. "And what's great about this punishment is that I can come back and make your life complete hell. Ain't that just fine and dandy, four eyes?"

Just then Jerry caught sight of his saviour – his own

superhero – Mr Finn.

"Aah, Mr Wayne Cadman is back with us, I see," the Deputy Head called out as he approached them. "And your friends have formed a welcome party to greet our eager scholars on this fresh Monday morning. How thoughtful of you."

To Jerry's amazement Wayno kept quiet and the gang all hung their heads in shame like berated toddlers. It took all Jerry's remaining energy to not burst out laughing.

"Young Mr Cadman, you seem to be forgetting out little appointment due five minutes ago; a little something called a readmission interview. Will your father be joining us?"

Wayno began shuffling unwillingly towards the imposing figure of the Deputy Head.

"No, sir. He said he had better things to do."

"Right then, let's get business started then. After you." He pointed in the direction of his office and watched Wayno saunter off a few paces.

"And the rest of you wave to the camera that's watching your every move." Mr Finn spun round dramatically and strode off, quickly catching up with Wayno who soon hurried to a trot behind him.

Jerry could only look on with awe.

Two of the lads sidled up to Jerry and talked under their breaths.

"You're dead meat, goggles."

They bumped Jerry with their shoulders to make known their intent and then unwillingly split away from their prey, walked back out of the school gates and round the corner to where the other smokers stood in groups coughing and sticking fingers up at the cars that hooted to them as they drove past.

To his surprise and amazement Silu, Matty and the others were not playing football in the usual place. Instead, he saw their goal being used by a bunch of year nines so Jerry decided to go to his locker.

He expected to see Silu in the locker area but only found a bunch of girls from his form group brushing their hair and comparing henna tattoos on their wrists and hands – the latest female craze.

"Hiya Jerry," one of the girls said, looking up and smiling.

He identified the voice as belonging to Chloe, who he knew to be one of Mindy's friends. Jerry smiled back.

"What are you lot up to here?"

"Usual girlie stuff," Chloe replied amicably. "Oi, Vikki. Come and show Jerry your piercing."

Vikki ambled over, chewing gum with an open mouth and brushing her bright red frizzy hair. She stood grinning in front of Jerry who wasn't sure where to look and couldn't see any piercing on her face or tongue. Then to his embarrassment she started to unbutton her blouse from the bottom and he wondered how far she was going to go. Luckily she stopped after two.

"Give me a drum roll, girlies," she said, grabbing the corners in each hand. "Ta da!" She pulled the blouse apart like a pair of stage curtains to display her podgy belly.

Jerry's initial reaction was one of horror. First her tummy protruded with a roll hanging indecorously over her skirt's waist band. Then his eyes felt compulsorily drawn towards the huge red blob where her belly button should have been. A small metal rod glinted in there somewhere, but its presence could not distract from the fact that all around it her skin looked bruised, blistered and even now still dotted with dried blood. Jerry felt physically sick.

"Cool," he said.

"Go, Vikki, my girlfriend," someone shouted in a bad American accent.

"You're one hot bitch, Vixen," called someone else.

Jerry felt out of his depth now and needed the reassurance of male company where he could get back to the safety of talking about football. But there was still no sign of Silu or Matty.

Registration was the normal chaos with Miss Powys. It became difficult to hear her when she attempted to speak as nobody stopped talking. The students didn't sit on chairs either, but ran around or lounged on desks. Jerry watched Miss Powys carefully, but she never once caught his eye. It so happened he had his tutor next for Citizenship – a daft lesson about quite irrelevant issues – and when the bell went he stayed in the room with Vikki and a boy called Stephen, a bit of a loner, who he'd only ever spoken to twice. Miss Powys disappeared briefly, promising to return very soon.

Sitting at his usual desk, Jerry watched Vikki scratch her belly and wince in silent agony, whilst Stephen slouched over his table, head laid upon folded arms. Then he heard the noise of approaching pupils and turned round to see a group of fellow classmates crowding through the door, including Silu and Matty among its number. Jerry waved with his right hand expecting Silu to come over and sit beside him as he always did in this lesson, but Silu seemed to look right through him and instead sat down on the other side of the room with Matty, who usually sat with Spencer. Unfazed, Spencer sat next to Vikki who began unbuttoning the bottom of her blouse for his close inspection of what was once her belly button.

Before the teacher returned the class became suddenly silent as the door crashed open.

"Where's that four-eyed fairy?" Wayno's voice boomed out.

Jerry's heart sank but he turned round in his chair to face his assailant.

"I've been told by old Quincy to leave you well alone. Why would that be then? Possibly because you're a sad little grass. If you think I'm gonna do what they tell me, you're wrong."

Wayno looked round the room like a victorious general after a battle surveying his newly conquered land.

"And don't think your so-called friends will help you." He stared at Silu and Matty and ran his index finger slowly across his throat. They looked away quickly.

A different voice intervened unexpectedly.

"Wayne Cadman, get to your own classroom now or I'll report you to Mr Finn immediately." It was Miss Powys.

"Okay miss, whatever you say. You're looking lovely today, miss. Well fit."

Miss Powys pushed past him and pointed out the door.

"Now!"

"I like a dominant woman, miss."

"Get out."

For some reason Wayno did as he was told without argument.

She smiled at Jerry before leaning against the teacher's desk where she opened her mark book containing her class registers. As she called out names, Jerry thought through the last few moments. Wayno was in the classroom next door, so he had about an hour of peace and quiet until it all kicked off again at break. He'd never expected to consider lessons in this way: as oases between the threats and kickings.

The period began well and sitting alone didn't feel so bad. In fact he felt under less pressure to pretend to be uninterested. There was nobody to talk to so he got on with the work set. At first Miss Powys led a short discussion during which he answered two questions for which he received more smiles. Then they were given a short assignment to write a police witness statement for a crime shown in obviously posed photos on the interactive whiteboard.

Then Jerry's class were disturbed by loud bangs, shouts and laughter from next door.

"What's that noise, miss?" asked Vikki.

Miss Powys looked up and tutted.

"There's a supply teacher next door. I imagine she's just discovered who Wayne Cadman is."

There came a titter of laughter from all except Jerry who groaned internally. His worst fears came to fruition when their classroom door opened to reveal a grey-haired, dishevelled little lady with a bright red face.

"Please can this rude, foul-mouthed boy sit at the back of your class?" she asked in an accent with a slight Germanic tinge. "I can tolerate him no longer. I have given him a detention. Where do I put the slip I have written out for that purpose?"

Miss Powys walked up to her and took the paper kindly. Jerry knew where he'd like to put it.

"I'll sort that out for you. Send him in." She patted the supply teacher on the arm in sympathy and support and held the door open for her to leave and for the ejected student to enter. It was of course Wayno.

"You're skating on very thin ice, boy." Miss Powys closed the door firmly and spoke directly to the lad even though she stood a good few inches shorter than him. He turned and squared up to her.

"Who are you calling 'boy'?"

"You, you silly little boy. Acting like a little baby. Would you like me to get your dummy, for you? What's wrong? Need to change your nappy?"

The class took in a deep synchronised breath. To everyone's amazement Wayno didn't retaliate. He huffed and looked round for support but found none. If anything he seemed to calm down slightly.

"What, you gonna change it for me, miss?" His scowl turned into a leer. "Don't mind you doing it, miss."

She turned away from him and began moving a chair and desk for him.

"Can't think of anything more revolting." She pulled the chair back. "Now sit down and shut up."

Wayno didn't move. Instead he looked around and grinned openly.

"It's alright, miss," he said with a nod of the head towards Jerry, "I'll sit over there, thanks."

"How dare you defy me! Do as I say right now or you will severely regret it!" Her explosion was unexpected but incredibly effective. "Do you understand how close you are to being permanently excluded? One word from me and we'll be seeing the back of you. Good riddance I say."

The class remained hushed in a squirming empathy.

With blatant reluctance, Wayno sat in the right chair, pushing the desk forward with a grating rasp. Miss Powys ignored him.

"Now then. Does everyone understand what they're doing? Good. Let's finish that quickly so we can move on to the next task. Let's say five more minutes. Have you got any work to be getting on with Wayne?"

She spent the next few minutes talking quietly to Wayno who eventually agreed to borrow a pen and at least write a few lines on a piece of paper. Jerry felt safely distanced enough from his persecutor to get his writing finished, although it remained hard to concentrate. Miss Powys did a good job distracting Wayno and for that Jerry was grateful.

Actually he felt sorry for his tutor, especially considering what he knew about her. Probably the last thing she wanted right now was some snivelling kid who thinks he's hard wasting her time and even making her uncomfortable by calling out rude comments.

The rest of the lesson passed uneventfully which came as something of a relief to all involved – except for one person. When the bell rang Miss Powys told everyone to stand behind their chairs. As they did so Jerry made the mistake of looking over at Wayno who made an aggressive twisting gesture and pointed starkly at him. Silu and Matty stared straight ahead of them and stood to attention behind their desks.

"Right then. When you're quiet you can go." The noise level sank to a low murmur. "Okay. Chairs under and I'll see you all next week. Tuck those shirts in, lads. Oh and Jerry Hough stay behind please, I need to speak to you. The rest of you go. Yes, that means you too, Wayne."

Once the hordes had dispersed and the class in the connected mobile had gone Miss Powys sat on a desk near to Jerry.

"Is that big oaf giving you trouble?"

"Wayno? Yeah," Jerry answered shame-facedly. "I was the reason he got suspended and he wants revenge."

"You should've told me before." Miss Powys screwed up her mouth in contemplation. "That's what tutors are for. I'm here to look out for you."

"Didn't you know?" Jerry assumed she knew about all the trouble.

"Nah, we're the last ones to be told. You pupils usually know these things way before we teachers find out what the heck is going on."

Jerry smiled amiably at this mild sign of frustration. He'd never really considered things much from a teacher's point of view before; after all aren't they just a bunch of sadists and androids whose express desire in life is to stop kids enjoying themselves?

"How much did you hear the other day?" she asked.

"Sorry, miss?"

"That day when you walked past me and I was on the phone." She suddenly looked up and grinned. "So, were you really bunking?"

"That was when I got beaten up. I'd had enough. It's a long story. You really didn't know?"

Miss Powys shook her head and bit her lip. "What a great tutor I am."

"You've got other things on your mind, miss."

"So you did hear?"

Jerry thought carefully before speaking again.

"It's your business, miss. I haven't said anything and I

promise not to. You have my word." Jerry could sense her discomfort as he spoke.

Miss Powys gave a quick smile as her eyes welled up and Jerry felt helpless in his concern. He couldn't exactly give her a hug.

"You're a great tutor, miss. And thanks for helping me out today with Wayno."

She leaned over and squeezed his arm. "That's okay Jerry. You're a good lad."

Just then a thudding sound came from the next room. Their mobile classroom was connected to one other and it sounded like someone moving about in there. Miss Powys put her finger to his lips and pointed melodramatically to the main door and with two fingers like a puppet she mimed walking in that direction. They both got up and exited the classroom into the shared lobby. Miss Powys opened the main external door, shared by both classrooms and ushered him out before quickly locking it.

Jerry's frown asked the question and Miss Powys giggled childishly.

"Wayne is in there. I watched him creep back in."

"What, you just locked him in?"

She nodded as her shoulders rocked with laughter.

"That gives you a head start. By the time he's realised and then used the fire exit the bell will have gone. What are you waiting for?"

Jerry wasted no time. He sped down the ramp and raced for cover.

Chapter Nine

At lunchtime, Jerry couldn't find Silu and the same year nines played on their pitch again. His final lesson was French and Jerry waited outside the class until Silu arrived in the corridor. As they always sat together nobody argued when Jerry took his arm and pushed him into his usual seat, making sure he sat next to him. Matty was in a different set.

"What the hell is going on?" Jerry sat down nudging him out of frustration. But Silu refused to talk. He'd only have a few seconds before Madame Coulson arrived and then there would certainly be no talking, except to answer her direct questions.

"Has he got to you? Is that it?"

Silu sat frozen as if hypnotised.

"Bonjour class!" sounded the sing-song voice.

Everyone dutifully stood up, scraping chairs.

"Bonn jaw Madam Coulson," they replied with very English accents in something distantly resembling unison.

The lesson began with a controlled 'discussion' and then the pupils had to fill in some tables with new vocabulary then design a word search puzzle using today's words.

As everyone scribbled, sucked pens, turned pages and coughed occasionally, Jerry gave up on his work and turned to the back page of his exercise book. He thought for a moment and then wrote something down

'*y r u ignoring me?*' He pushed the book over onto Silu's work after checking the teacher wasn't looking.

Silu simply pushed the book back.

65

Jerry refused to give up.

'*r u scared of wayno?*'

Wearily, Silu leaned over and wrote a short reply.

'*sod off*'

'*that's a yes then*'

'*just leave us alone were not your friends any more*'

'*did he tell u 2 say that?*'

'*FU 4 eyes*'

Jerry sat back in his chair: that one hurt.

"Monsieur Hough, move your things to the front desk. Immediatement!"

As he collected his equipment Silu refused to look at him.

At home time Silu mysteriously disappeared and as Jerry walked out the gate he spotted Matty, who instantly turned up his collar and switched direction like a corny private eye. Jerry sighed. Instead he pressed his mp3 player's earphones into his ears, pushed play and strode onwards. As he walked he felt tempted to remove his glasses to see the effect it had. He would of course have to be careful when crossing roads but he knew the journey well enough to be confident he could manage it.

As soon as he'd removed his glasses that same swirling haze appeared. Yet this time he noticed it wasn't just a general mist but a specifically localised one for which Jerry could define the edges or borders. It took on a specific shape then after a few minutes came apart to regroup into a different form. It was translucent enough for him to be able to see his way forward and to avoid obstacles or other people in his path. The haze actually seemed to improve his eyesight, as if it were a lens to look through sharpening his vision.

Just then the sun came out – he could feel its warmth on the back of his neck and head. He spotted his own shadow looming up before him on the pavement, bobbing and dancing in tempo with his own movements. As Jerry strode forwards 'in sync' with his shadow he walked past a lamppost which dissected his dark double through the midriff and made it instantly disappear as if sliced in two and evaporated. He looked again. No shadow existed even though the sun shone warmly over him.

Jerry looked back instinctively, squinting into the sun, and became aware of a few unidentified people a little way behind him. He turned back to see that his shadow had reappeared: or rather, not his shadow. For the dark shape projected on the path before him was certainly not his own.

Jerry checked behind again but nobody stood near him, just those two or three about twenty metres away so it had nothing to do with them. He walked on, once again aware of his poor vision which couldn't focus on very much ahead. However, when he looked at the shadow again the dark mass stood out clearly focussed which explained why his eyes were drawn to its attractive clarity.

Maybe it was his shadow after all, Jerry mused. Just not quite how he expected it to look. Further examination as he continued to walk on, allowed him to discern the outline. It was him. The shadow's arms moved when Jerry moved them. But the main difference was that the shadow wore a hat – or more properly a helmet with a plume of feathers. His usually wiry frame looked massive as if he wore armour plating with hands in gauntlets. Raising his right hand it didn't surprise him this time to see that its shadowed counterpart gripped a huge broadsword. The wide girth of his alternate body could be explained by the fact that he wasn't actually walking but riding a large creature – the black unicorn.

Just as he began to enjoy the fantasy a loud volley of giggles interrupted his music and dispelled the image. He quickly pulled out his earphones. At first he didn't want to look behind for fear of confronting Wayno, but when he heard a voice he recognised he turned sharply and saw that a small group of figures walked closely behind him.

"What's he doing now, exactly?" an unfamiliar female voice asked.

"Looks like he was pretending to ride a horse," a different female voice replied. "Your boyfriend seems a bit … um … weird."

"Stop it girls," Mindy answered. "He isn't my boyfriend." Jerry felt a bit hurt by this as she said it with a definite air of certainty.

Jerry stopped in his tracks and fumbled for his glasses. Mindy walked in between three of her school friends. He recognised one as Chloe from his form group.

"Hiya ladies."

He enjoyed being greeted by four friendly smiles – something he hadn't experienced for a while.

"Hello Jerry." Mindy caught up with him and linked her arm in his. Chloe did the same on the other side and Jerry felt a thrill as he allowed himself to be escorted in this way.

"So is it official then? You're all my stalkers?"

The four girls giggled and Mindy pushed her elbow into his ribs amicably.

"Kayleigh here lives nearby and we're going to hers."

Jerry looked behind and recognised Kayleigh as someone he often saw on the bus.

"You like walking, eh?" said Kayleigh. Jerry nodded. "I see you when I go past in the bus."

"Yeah, I like the exercise," Jerry explained. "And the chance to be quiet and think. Or listen to music. You know – personal time."

The four girls murmured assent.

"Well you did say he was fit," Chloe said with a grin.

"Hmm - fit and brave. Quite a combination." Mindy looked straight at him as she spoke.

"So where do you live, Mindy?" Jerry felt confidence oozing within him.

"Tilgate. Just by the park."

This was good news as he could cycle to the park in about ten minutes from his home.

"Oh, I really like Tilgate Park," Jerry said. "I like all the animals in the nature centre."

"We should meet down there some time."

"Yeah, we should. I'd like that." Jerry felt something stick in his throat which made his voice wobble slightly, but he reckoned he just about got away with it.

"We're nearly at your place, Jerry," Mindy said, slowing down as they came to a crossroads.

"How do you know where I live?"

"Oh, um, Kayleigh told me," Mindy added quickly.

"Yeah, that's right. I often see you walking down there." Kayleigh spoke quickly, covering for her friend.

"So what you doing on Saturday?" Jerry stepped into dangerously new territory here. He remained confident as long as he imagined himself the champion knight of Myopia. All the damsels swooned when he walked by.

"Nothing," Mindy replied; her brown eyes looking into his encouragingly.

"Do you fancy hanging out somewhere?"

"We could meet in town?" she suggested.

"I'll pick you up."

"What? In your stretched Limo?"

"No, on my unicorn," Jerry countered without thinking. "And we'll ride off into the sunset."

The group of girls giggled.

"Unicorn?" Chloe snorted.

Mindy looked at Jerry bemused. "I like you, Jerry, even though you seem slightly disturbed at times. But it makes you unpredictable and I like that in a man." She gave her friends a hard stare until they stopped whispering and nudging each other. Then she turned back to Jerry. "Give me your phone."

Jerry did as he was told. Mindy flipped it open and began tapping in some information. She closed it and threw it back.

Luckily he caught it.

"See you, Jerry. Come on girls." The four girls spun round and walked away in a conspiratorial huddle, never once looking back.

Once they'd disappeared he continued trudging homewards, when he remembered to look at his phone. In the address book just before 'mum' there shone out in all rapturous letters the name 'Mindy ;)'. He tried to work out if the little winking smiley was suggestive in any way. Then he got neurotic and worried it might be a joke, so he checked to see it did lead to a number. Was it genuine? She might have put in a false one. But why would she do that? It didn't make sense. He considered calling her right now to check it but that would make him look a bit sad and desperate. Better to make her wait. That made him look a bit cooler, he surmised. He'd have to hang on until tomorrow and make it sound really casual.

During that evening he constantly checked his address book to make sure the numbers hadn't melted off the screen.

As he lay in bed, thinking about her beautiful eyes and hair and trying to remember the exact words of their conversation today, he caved in and sent her a text.

'hi mindy just checking the number works hope ur ok c ya tomorrow'.

When he received no reply he started losing confidence and wished he hadn't been so weak. He felt he'd failed his first test and wanted someone to explain the rules. It seemed all so unnecessarily complicated. The night passed gloomily: sleepless but uneventful.

The next day was Friday and Mindy still hadn't replied. That's that then, thought Jerry: the shortest relationship in the history of the universe.

Once again none of his football mates could be seen in the playground and it seemed they'd lost their spot as some year elevens now used it for basketball. He went to his locker to sort out his stuff for the day. Then Jerry saw something he never thought he'd see. Wayno's gang were doing their usual marauding through the corridors and when they saw Jerry they cheered and ran up to him. At the back of the huddling gang he recognised two faces more clearly than the others: Silu and Matty. They tried to look like they weren't part of the horde but they obviously had become hangers-on. It was true, if hard to believe.

Wayno's usual taunts went unheard as Jerry tried to get eye-contact with his two friends – or ex-friends. They refused to look up and Jerry felt angry that they should give in so easily.

"Can I try on your new space visors?"

Jerry groaned inwardly. These glasses had only lasted a week or so and were about to be broken already. He looked around for help but Vicki and Chloe could only offer a sympathetic look. Instead assistance came from a disembodied voice.

"I'm going to count to five and if after that time there is anybody hanging around who does not have a locker here then you'll be paying Mr Finn a visit."

Amazingly the whole gang scarpered like mischievous toddlers.

Miss Powys appeared as if by magic, looking round with a serious expression.

"My lot – you have two minutes to get to the form room. Anyone late will get a lunchtime detention."

Everyone filed out quietly as Miss Powys held the door. She refused to smile at Jerry who thanked her as he shuffled past.

After school Jerry hung around to watch the year 10 football match against Dovecote Hall, the local private school.

Silu was captain and Matty played on the left wing. Rhino also made the team, bolstering up the defence with his stocky frame. The game was a poor one. The home team didn't retain the ball and had to defend the waves of attacks mounted by Dovecote, who possessed some tricksy players. Inevitably, the away team scored, but all it really achieved was to make Rhino angry. Unfortunately he lost all self-control.

The Dovecote centre forward made a great run through the middle of the field skipping over tacklers until he only had Rhino and the goalie to beat. Cleverly slotting the ball through Rhino's legs didn't turn out to be such a wise move as the big defender stuck out an arm which swiftly looped around the striker's neck until he'd wrestled him to the floor. Once beneath him, Rhino began pounding his opponent's face until it took three teachers to drag him away and restrain him. The match was abandoned with Dovecote taking the three points to put them top of the local league. An ambulance arrived, its wheels skidding on the muddy pitch and spectators were ushered out the gates and sent home. Somehow the local press arrived and were soon chasing after the ambulance. It was quite a scene.

Jerry tried to talk to Silu again but he and Matty walked past and got into Silu's dad's car without offering him a lift. Jerry began his walk home as the street lights began to flicker on. At least it was Friday and tomorrow held an exciting and new experience in store for him. He checked his mobile to see whether her number was still in there.

A text message waited for him: '*47 Parkside Terrace 10.30*'.

Chapter Ten

The door was opened by a tall man in a suit. He had strikingly handsome features framed by dark, greying hair. The man stepped forwards with his right hand held out in greeting.

"You must be the famous Jerry?"

"Hello, Mr Sidhu. Nice to meet you." He nervously lifted his own hand which was quickly enveloped and squeezed. Mr Sidhu kept hold of his hand and grasped Jerry's elbow with his other, gently pulling him inside the house.

"Come on in and make yourself at home, Jerry." Mr Sidhu finally released his young guest and directed him into the living room. For a small terraced house it was certainly ornately furnished, with its red leather sofa, deep-pile purple and gold carpet; antique mahogany table; bookcases full of leather-bound volumes; and uncountable candles and figurines. The walls were covered with what looked like Arabian flying carpets, but pride of place in the middle wall hung a gigantic painting of an elephant-headed god.

"Is that Ganesh?" Jerry asked, hoping he hadn't offended his friendly hosts. He remembered the name from an RS lesson on Hinduism.

Mr Sidhu clapped his hands together. "Yes, isn't he wonderful? He is the storyteller and what is life but a series of stories? That painting was done by my great-grandfather who was a renowned artist in old Bengal."

"Jasbir, let the young man sit down," said a voice from behind them. "He doesn't want to hear about your family of beggars."

Jerry turned round to see an older version of Mindy. She wore a tracksuit and trainers and was tying up her long black hair in a ponytail.

"Hello, Jerry. Excuse me won't you but I'm just off out for a jog. I hope we can have a proper chat another time. Don't let Jasbir bore your pants off with tedious stories about how poor his family used to be or you'll never get away. Parminder will be down in a sec. See ya."

Mr Sidhu beckoned to the sofa with a smile.

"Excuse my wife, Jerry, she has a bit of a fitness obsession. But I have to say she does keep in fine shape and has a lovely figure for a woman of her age, don't you think?"

Jerry would have preferred to think about Mindy's figure but assumed it best not to say so in front of her father.

"Now then," Mr Sidhu continued. "You just have enough time to try one of Kamala's samosas."

"No dad, we're going out now."

There in the doorway stood Mindy buttoning up her coat. She had black jeans and a pair of suede boots on which made her look even taller and more leggy than usual.

"But I was just getting to know your gentleman caller," Mr Sidhu gave Jerry a mischievous wink. "Ah, the youth of today. Always in a rush and no respect for their parents."

"Yeah, whatever, Dad. We'll be having lunch out so don't wait for me. Be back later this afternoon."

The idea of lunch out was a welcome surprise to Jerry and he made what he hoped was a polite shrug to Mindy's dad.

"Better not keep the memsahib waiting," Mr Sidhu said out the corner of his mouth. "She has quite a temper on her." Here he nudged Jerry and whispered loudly. "Gets it from her mother."

"Come on Jerry," Mindy said with a deep breath of exasperation and moving off towards the front door.

"Stand up for yourself, son. You don't want to end up a gibbering wreck like me." Mr Sidhu proceeded to feign a nervous twitch and held out a shaking hand for Jerry to inspect.

"Ignore my dad, he thinks he's funny. Let's go." She linked her arm in Jerry's and walked out the door leaving Mr Sidhu to wave them off.

"Don't turn around and encourage him or he'll think you like him," Mindy said sternly.

"Your dad's cool."

"You don't have to live with him."

They took the bus and sat upstairs, getting off outside County Mall. He wanted everyone from school to see him with her. Accompanying her to shops as she tried on tops and skirts was a new experience for him; even just sitting patiently outside changing rooms became something he wanted to savour.

For lunch they found the food hall. Jerry chose a burger meal in the end whilst Mindy, who he discovered to be a vegetarian, selected a jacket potato and salad. Whilst it was noisy with lots of toddlers haring about and screaming at the tops of their voices, neither minded as they enjoyed each other's company. Once they'd finished, Jerry cleared their table then bought them some coffees.

"So what do you fancy doing this afternoon?" he asked as he poured her a second cup from the cafetiere.

"Well, I'm looking for a new top and some shoes."

"Haven't you already bought two tops?" Jerry furrowed his brow.

"You can never have too many tops," Mindy replied with no hint of irony. "What about you? Are you looking for anything?"

"Oh, DVDs and stuff."

"Oh, okay. We could split up and meet again later."

"No, no. I'm more than happy to be with you." Jerry tried to speak without too much panic in his voice. "Anyway you need me to carry your bags."

"So I do. And you make such a good beast of burden."
Mindy reached over and patted his hand.

"Exactly," said Jerry, relieved. He hoped she was joking although being insulted by Mindy was preferable to most other pastimes he could imagine.

"Your parents seem really nice," Jerry said, hoping he could get to know all the family better.

"I suppose so," Mindy relented. "Mum's a bit like a best friend and Dad had a really tough childhood."

"What? In Bengal?"

"No. Crawley actually."

"Oh, sorry. I didn't mean ..." Jerry floundered, annoyed with himself for being so stupid. "That sounded like really crass stereotyping. I'm sorry I ..."

Luckily, Mindy laughed. "It's ok – I know you didn't mean anything by it. No, he was bullied. A lot. You see, he was the only non-white kid in his class. He got beaten, teased and spat on, but he always refused to fight back. He always taught me that the most important thing in life is to keep your dignity and self-respect. We should dust ourselves down and keep on walking with our heads held high."

"Good advice." Jerry stared at her, nodding. "Your Dad is awesome."

"Anyway, I know what it's like," Mindy continued. "'Paki' is not much different to 'Four Eyes'. It's something I've had all my life; just have to get immune to it. Those bigoted idiots need to look beyond the skin."

"And beyond the glasses," Jerry added.

Their eyes met as they nodded in agreement.

They finished their coffees and Jerry gathered up the bags, splitting them into two lots, equally weighted. However the bags in his left hand proved much heavier with one of the plastic handles cutting into his fingers; but he refused to complain.

He followed Mindy as she strode off in search of the perfect bargain. A couple of times he lost sight of her completely and at one point he considered phoning her as he felt stupid in the middle of the shop getting in everyone's way. She reappeared eventually after about quarter of an hour, tapping him on the shoulder and he turned to see her wearing different clothes.

"What do you think?"

Her top was a blue and yellow, summery, strappy item which showed off her figure in the most flattering way he could imagine. When she moved he could see her belly button. Below that she wore stone-washed jeans cropped below the knees, showing her shapely legs, ending in dark, heeled shoes that made her taller than him. She looked about twenty five.

"Wow!" Jerry blew outwards in astonishment.

"Does that mean you like it?"

"You look amazing. I mean really ... lovely."

"Oh, I'm glad you like it. This top is only ten quid."

The price meant nothing to him. He was surprised it cost that much to be honest as it didn't involve a great deal of material.

"Should I buy the whole outfit?"

Jerry wasn't so sure about the shoes, which Silu would have called 'bitch-pumps', but he knew better than to say so.

"You look exquisite."

"Exquisite, eh? I like that." Mindy did a spin for him looking pleased with his assessment. "I'll take that as a yes then."

It took another twenty minutes for her to change and then queue up to pay but he stood patiently until she returned with a beaming smile on her face.

Eventually they got to W H Smith which had a music and film section. As he flicked through the DVDs he became aware of Mindy looking bored but he decided to ignore her. When she tapped his shoulder and said his name he felt annoyed at her impatience.

"Just a few more minutes …"

"Jerry!" Mindy's voice sounded urgent. Jerry stopped and looked up in the direction her eyes were darting.

"Oh no!"

"Why, it's none other than my four-eyed fairy."

Wayno strutted right up to Jerry, scanning him closely from head to his toe. A group of his cronies stood off at a distance nudging each other.

"You're looking under the wrong section for ballet and princesses. You'll need the four-eyed fairy freak department over there."

This elicited a volley of guffaws from his mob.

Then Wayno spotted Mindy for the first time and looked genuinely taken aback.

"Don't tell me you're with him?"

Both Mindy and Jerry remained silent and still.

"What is that all about? Are you taking the mick or what?" He moved over to Mindy and put his hand on her waist. "Don't waste your time with this joker, babe. I'll show you what it's like to be with a real man."

Jerry couldn't speak or move. He was the proverbial bunny in the spotlight: a fluffy, wet-nosed, baby-faced wimp. He hated himself.

Mindy pushed Wayno away.

"Sod off, Wayno."

"What the hell are you doing with him?"

"Shopping."

Jerry winced. The word had just slipped out. He couldn't really answer Wayno's question, especially as he had spent the entire day wondering exactly the same thing himself.

Wayno stepped up to him until their noses touched.

"Think you're so bloody hard don't you?"

His breath reeked of stale fags.

Then Jerry felt a sharp pain on his forehead and stepped back, reeling. It took him a few seconds to realise what had happened. Wayno had head-butted him. Mindy squealed; Wayno stood his ground grinning, then a man moved quickly towards them.

"Hey, you there. What's going on?"

The deep adult voice put things back into perspective and had an effect on Wayno and his crew. They suddenly shot away, making for the nearest exit, leaving the man in two minds. By which time they'd disappeared.

"You okay, son?"

The man, clearly some kind of a security guard, spoke rapidly into his walkie-talkie.

"Four or five lads just run out of Smiths – anyone see 'em? Get back to me."

He put a hand under Jerry's chin to check his face.

"Gonna have a nice bruise there tomorrow, son. Who was that?"

"Dunno. He just started having a go at me."

Mindy came over, visibly shaking. "He was asking for money but Jerry refused to give him any."

"Probably on drugs or something." The security guard sniffed. "Do you want me to call the police or take you home, or something?"

"No, thanks. I'm fine."

Mindy put an arm round him. "I'll take him for a coffee."

"Looks like he needs something stronger," the security guard chuckled.

"Thanks for your help," Mindy said. She put an arm round Jerry's shoulders and walked him to the door which led back out to the mall.

"Watch out for concussion," the man added helpfully. "Look after him now." The security man held the door open before speaking into his walkie-talkie again.

That last phrase resonated for Jerry who felt particularly stupid at this moment. He'd just been assaulted and was being helped by a girl he'd just spent the day hoping to impress.

Maybe Wayno was right. He was just a sad little four-eyed freak. Mindy could do so much better, so why was he fooling himself and wasting her time?

"Where shall we go for a drink?" Mindy asked him gently.

"Home," Jerry mumbled.

"Oh, are you sure? It might be good to sit down somewhere." Mindy suggested. "You need something with sugar."

"I'm fine. I just want to go home."

"Let's get a taxi then."

"You can stay in town, if you want to. I'll walk home," Jerry insisted.

"No, I won't let you. If you go then I will too."

"I'll walk you home then."

"This is silly," Mindy said with concern.

"So I'll just have to be silly." Jerry knew he was being difficult and sullen but he wanted to get away from Mindy and be on his own.

"Let's get the bus at least. Please, Jerry."

The thought of sitting down for a bit did appeal to Jerry.

"Okay," he said sulkily.

They caught the bus to Mindy's house, sitting together in silence for the entire journey. At the stop they got off together and Jerry did the decent thing and walked her to her house.

"Come in and have some hot chocolate and one of mum's famous samosas. Please." She gave a pleading smile.

Jerry shook his head and turned away when he felt his eyes welling up.

"See you on Monday," he croaked then slowly trudged away without looking back.

During the whole walk home he repeated a mantra under his breath in time to his footsteps: "Stupid saddo four-eyed freak, stupid saddo four-eyed freak, stupid..."

Chapter Eleven

Jerry didn't feel like the champion of Myopia any more. He didn't deserve someone as lovely as Mindy; girls like her only went out with other guys. And how he hated Wayno.

The next few nights he couldn't sleep because his mind became invaded with scenarios in which he confronted the bully and smashed his teeth in. Although vaguely aware of a swirling mist and a spiral haze as he stared up at the ceiling, he put the phenomenon down to his own insanity and insomnia. Jerry felt a desperate urge and desire to sleep but his ridiculous brain would not let him. Instead he lay there for hours upon hours making up conversations, reviewing and analysing every action and word said both by him and to him.

He should have stood up for Mindy and himself instead of just clamming up and shutting down. Maybe he needed to go the gym or take up boxing and finally learn how to defend himself. A growing awareness of his own wimpiness began to irritate him. What a stupid, wet mummy's-boy he must seem to everyone. No wonder Silu and Matty wanted nothing to do with him. It made him cringe to think he was one of those saddoes with the word 'victim' written across his face. Probably near the lump he still had on his forehead from being head-butted.

Eventually, as the light began to show through the curtains a constantly changing shadow which seemed small and close one second then large and far away the next, become a soothing comfort to him as he watched its malleable shape ebbing and flowing. His brain became less active and the shadow descended upon him like a blanket to smother his fears and give his brain a much needed release from his worries and fears. He drifted into the happy place he called Myopia.

When his dad woke him up at the usual time on Monday morning Jerry had resolved a number of things. He was going to attempt to get round school without his glasses. The place must surely be familiar enough for him to find his various classrooms without them. In lessons he could wear them to help him see the board, books or screen. Break and lunchtime could prove more problematic.

Once he'd left the house and turned the corner Jerry removed his glasses and folded them into a hard, black case which he put into his blazer pocket. It came as no surprise when the mist appeared before him. Rather than being an obstacle it seemed to be pointing the way and helping to clarify objects. Could a shadowy blob really be helping him or was this yet another sign of his own slow descent into insanity?

He made it safely to school with no comments from the other pupils he passed on the way. Just inside the gates he became aware of the usual gangs and cliques: the smokers, the dealers, the loud-mouths, and that group of girls who liked hanging round the street corner practising for their future profession in soliciting. Amazingly he made it through without a problem or insult – possibly because nobody recognised him.

Suddenly he heard a shout which he thought he recognised as Silu's voice. Looking round was a bit pointless as he couldn't see much further than his outstretched hand, but he instinctively seemed to know which direction the sound came from. He picked up his pace to a run until he reached the group of boys from whom the shout had come. The first person he recognised was Matty who turned to him with a look of panic. No one else looked up from the crowd. In the middle Jerry heard again Silu's cries of anguish. Jerry knew he had to help his mate.

Head down, Jerry shoulder-barged into the group, scattering a few boys onto the floor. This got him quickly into the centre of the action. There in the middle were two bodies wrestling in the dirt. Wayno was pushing Silu's head back and he looked in a great deal of agony. Then without further thought Jerry flung himself on Wayno and rolled him off the grateful Silu.

The surprise of the attack gave Jerry an advantage. Before Wayno could work out what had happened Jerry slammed his fist into the bully's nose. Jerry recoiled from the searing agony in his hand. It felt like he'd broken his fingers. The punch seemed to have done the trick though as Wayno sprawled on the floor holding his face.

With his still blurry vision, Jerry wasn't sure whether the red all over Wayno's hands and face was blood or just an illusion caused by his own anger.

Jerry walked off without being stopped.

In the locker area, news had spread quickly and Jerry found himself greeted by a clamour of questions and shouting.

"Was there a fight?"

"Tell us what happened."

"Did you punch Wayno?"

"Have we missed all the action?"

"Did he get you?"

"That guy had it coming to him."

"What did it feel like?"

"It bloody well hurt," Jerry replied unable to bend his knuckle without considerable pain. A bruise already began to show.

"Did you really get him?"

"How did it start?"

But Jerry didn't feel like answering them. He wanted to be alone.

In the mobile classroom he found Stephen, which ruined his plan somewhat. Stephen looked up from his book.

"Fighting is never the answer, you know."

Jerry stood back in amazement.

"What did you say?"

"An eye for an eye makes the whole world blind."

"What the hell are you on about?" Jerry knew his voice sounded aggressive, but it was only in response to Stephen's smugness.

"It was Mahatma Ghandi who said that. Violence only leads to further violence." Stephen went back to his book and Jerry stood silent and still in amazement.

"And I think it was Confucius," Stephen continued undeterred, "who rightly stated, 'He who looks for revenge should dig himself two graves.'"

"What the sodding heck are you chatting about?" Jerry could feel an irrational anger rising within him. "Are you looking for a slap?"

"What? No." Stephen gave a look of confusion. As Jerry advanced towards him the look changed to one of fear. "Honestly I was just trying to help you. I know you're not a bad guy, but you mustn't let yourself become like him..."

"Who the hell do you think you're talking to?" Jerry asked in a raise voice.

"We're the same," Stephen said, flinching as Jerry grabbed hold of his collar. "You and me. I understand what you're going through."

"The same?" shouted Jerry, pulling Stephen out of his chair. "We're not the bloody same." Jerry then shoved Stephen over the desk and raised his right arm, ignoring the pain induced by clenching his fist. "I'm not a snivelling, saddo, little loner. I'm not the same as you."

Jerry's fingers throbbed and itched to pound the life out of Stephen. The wrath within him became a monster that overwhelmed his body and mind – a blood-lust. Looking at Stephen through his aching eyes and with a headache beating at his temples, Jerry imagined this face as Wayno's, and his dream about putting his fist through his skull and teeth flashed before him. He felt a great urge to hurt him, someone, anyone …

"Jerry! No! Stop now!"

The new voice had an effect on Jerry, who uncurled his fist and dropped hold of Stephen.

Miss Powys grabbed Jerry's arm and pushed him roughly away from Stephen, towards the door.

"God, I expected better from you of all people." Her facial expression displayed a mixture of shock and disappointment.

Jerry pulled away from her and felt ashamed.

"You're already in a lot of trouble, Jerry. Mr Finn wants to see you in his office and it's not looking good. This sort of rubbish is only going to make it worse." She turned away from him. "Are you okay, Stephen?"

Stephen sat back down, nodding and picked up his book again.

"Sorry, Stephen," Jerry muttered. "I didn't mean to hurt you."

"It's all right, Jerry. It's okay, miss. I think I understand."

"Still no excuse for that kind of behaviour," Miss Powys shook her head as she sat at her desk and unpacked her books. "Mr Finn told me what happened, Jerry. Why'd you do it?"

"Wayno was beating up Silu."

Miss Powys nodded. "Well you'd better see what Mr Finn has to say about it all. Have you calmed down now? Tuck your shirt in and be polite to him. Go on, get off with you."

"Yes miss." Jerry turned to leave.

"Jerry," Miss Powys called. He stopped with one hand on the door frame. "Good luck, eh?"

Jerry smiled and left the mobile, pushing past the mob now arriving for registration.

"Then you are a complete idiot, boy." Mr Finn was not known for his subtlety. "Violence is never the answer."

"He was hurting my best mate."

"But that is not the way to deal with it, Jerry. Why get yourself in trouble? What should you have done?"

Jerry repressed the sigh building up within him. "I should've told someone."

"Right. It's not 'grassing up' – it's doing the right thing." Finn loomed over Jerry; it seemed the only way they could both fit in this small office.

"But I did that last time and nothing's changed."

"Excuse me? Wayne Cadman was suspended," Mr Finn replied in a slightly hurt tone.

"Yeah but he came back and carried on exactly the same."

Mr Finn sighed and looked out of the window. "I know. If it was up to me I'd kick the little hooligan out immediately. Ruining everyone else's education and making life a misery for everyone – including the teachers. There are always one or two who spoil things for everybody else. Unfortunately there's something called 'social inclusion' which makes it damn nigh impossible to get the buggers out these days." He stopped, worried he'd said too much. "And now you have a problem because nobody is willing to give a witness report to say Cadman hit your friend, including your friend himself – um, Sachindra Patel, is it?"

"Yeah, Silu we call him."

"Well that's bad news for you as there are lots of witnesses who say your attack was unprovoked."

"But they're lying," Jerry insisted, aware that his voice sounded strained. "Or they're scared of Wayno."

"Possibly," Mr Finn nodded with one eyebrow raised in deep contemplation. "But you have to understand the difficult situation that puts us in. It's now your word against a dozen or so others."

"But if you check our records, sir, to see who is more likely to be telling the truth…"

"I have checked your record, Jerry. And whilst it generally

shows a clean track-record there are a few misdemeanours creeping in of late that you need to iron out. You've been caught truanting on at least one occasion. Some teachers, when I asked them, have said your homework recently has not been of the best quality. Mr Platt especially has a few choice things to say about you. It seems neither you nor your father endeared yourselves to him."

"Yes, but Mr Platt is a ..."

"Now, now, Jerry." Mr Finn allowed himself a frown and Jerry knew to shut up. "I expect better from you. It's no good blaming others. You have to start taking responsibility for your own actions. It's important to get on with your Head of Year and when you return I expect you to make some reparation to that relationship. He's an important figure in your education and you will show him the due respect that his position holds. Is that clear?"

"Yes, sir."

Mr Finn stood up and the top of his head nearly hit the ceiling. He blocked the window, leaving Jerry in his gloomy corner.

"Now that leaves us with this latest incident. You have put a boy in hospital, Jerry, which makes this a very serious issue."

Jerry's heart leapt. Hospital? He wanted to hear Finn say it again. Little him had put Wayno in hospital? No wonder his fingers hurt so much.

"Is Wayno okay?"

Mr Finn stared at Jerry through narrowed eyes before looking away and smiling to himself.

"Fractured nose and ten stitches on the lip I heard. Poor lamb." He checked Jerry again, suppressing another laugh. "Couldn't have happened to a nicer guy."

Jerry held his nose as snorting with laughter in front of Finn would have been bad form.

"But anyway, this is a serious issue." Mr Finn broke in with a deeper tone. "I'm afraid, after consultation with the Head and Mr Platt, that we have no option other than to exclude you from school for two days. That's school policy and the Governors, I'm sure, will ratify it. So we need to speak to your parents. Who would you prefer us to call? Mum or dad?"

Jerry shrugged. It made no difference as he would have to explain it all to both of them any way.

"Then I'll speak to your father. I'd like to meet him after all I've heard about him. Sounds like an interesting chap." Finn nodded to himself and Jerry hoped he'd be able to witness this rendezvous between two great men.

"Now then, Jerry. Is there anything else you would like to know before we send you home?"

Pouting slightly, Jerry shook his head. Finn looked disappointed.

"Well, I have one thing to say to you."

Jerry braced himself for a lecture or a blasting.

"I thought you'd like to know that whilst Cadman was grassing you up – and according to him you are the biggest bully in the school – whilst he dobbed you in he blubbed like the big baby he really is. Just thought I'd share that image with you."

Finn stood up and opened the door. "Wait out here for your dad to collect you. God bless, son."

He didn't get to witness the great meeting but there seemed to be much hilarity between Finn and his Dad, especially for a disciplinary hearing. When the door finally opened Mr Hough smiled and beckoned to Jerry.

"Come on then, knuckles. Let's get you home." Jerry's dad then walked down the corridor to the car whistling merrily.

As he got into the car, Jerry wondered what Finn had told his dad.

"You know I'm suspended?"

"Oh yeah, but Mr Finn – he's a good bloke, eh? Turns out he's a rock climber too – he explained all the circumstances. Sounds like this other guy deserved it. If I ever meet him I'll bust his other lip."

Mr Hough faced Jerry before turning the ignition and patted him on the knee.

"Didn't know you had it in you, son."

Jerry smiled, but didn't feel particularly satisfied. To him it didn't feel like he'd really won a victory but rather had exacerbated the conflict further. He tried to remember what Stephen had said about 'an eye for an eye'.

Chapter Twelve

Aware of his parents chatting as they got up he decided to rise and make the most of his first day at home. Jerry looked around the room without his glasses and thought he could make out some of the familiar blurs and general haze.

His parents' voices got louder and clearer.

"Why not this weekend?" Mrs Hough sounded exasperated.

"Cos I'm off with Danny to try that new climbing wall. I told you a million times."

"Not all day surely?"

"Yeah, but then it's the footie." Mr Hough's voice became strained too. Jerry sighed.

"Well what about Sunday?"

"Big Frank isn't around. I need him to help with that huge main bough and the secondary lower limb – can't do that on my own."

"Well, when then?" Mrs Hough began stacking pots and plates which Jerry knew she did when really rattled. "That flippin' tree is going to smash our house to pieces before you get organised. I've half a mind to get another firm in to do it."

"Oi! You dare. I'll talk to the lads today." The following silence told Jerry that his mum was now giving his dad the silent treatment.

After washing and dressing quickly he found his mobile and wrote a text: '*sorry bout other day how r u*'. Then he selected Mindy's number and sent it before he could talk himself out of doing so. After waiting a few moments for a reply, he assumed she might not be up yet or was too busy getting ready. Perhaps she hadn't even switched her phone on yet.

Downstairs, his mum and dad had begun breakfast.

"I still can't believe our boy's been suspended from school." Mrs Hough said with a tone of regret. "What are we going to do about this bullying?" Even though he stood in the room they talked as if he wasn't there. "Do we need to go into school and talk to someone?"

"No, it's being dealt with." Mr Hough chuckled. "Believe me, that Mr Finn will sort it out in no time."

"But bullies don't stop just because they've been ticked off by a teacher. What if they carry on making Jerry's life a misery?"

"Then I'll teach Jerry how to defend himself. It's about time."

"I wish you'd told us earlier, Jerry." Mrs Hough finally acknowledged his presence. "I thought we could talk about things?" Her eyes welled up as she spoke.

"I was a bit embarrassed I suppose," Jerry replied.

"Yeah, but you showed him, eh?" said his dad. "What was it? Fractured nose and stitches in the lip?"

Jerry started to smile as he remembered the image of Wayno blubbing like a baby.

"No, that's not a good thing at all," his mum insisted. "That makes you as bad as him…"

"Grief, hardly!" Mr Hough exclaimed. "I think breaking his lip is completely justified," his dad said unexpectedly.

Jerry couldn't help agreeing with his mum. He didn't feel proud of it and his biggest concern was the repercussion when he returned. His mum obviously had the same thought.

"So what happens when this guy comes back to school? What about his mates? As far as I can see you've just created even more trouble."

Jerry nodded. "And my hand really hurts too."

"I'll get you some paracetamol."

His worrying continued into the night, stopping him from sleeping properly. The whole situation with Wayno was stupid. The only reason that idiot picked on him was because he wore glasses – something Jerry had no control over.

In the darkness and without his glasses he became aware, once more, of the hazy mist. He put out a hand to feel if he could touch the haze. To his surprise (or was it just his imagination?) his fingers seemed to go clammy with a subtle lowering of the temperature and the air became palpably moist.

"Hello?" he said to the mist. When no reply came Jerry felt incredibly stupid. He couldn't explain the weird phenomena caused by his myopia, but one thing did occur to him: perhaps short-sightedness was not a disability after all, but rather a way of seeing the world in a different way.

"But there must be no hate, Jerry," Mr Finn stated firmly. "You must overcome all anger and hatred and any thought of revenge."

"It's hard not to hate Wayno," Jerry admitted.

"Something else I've learnt from my vast experience is that bullying just creates more bullies, like perpetual motion. One person bullies two others then they go off and bully two people each and so on. If you know anything about maths then you'll realise the numbers become very big quite quickly."

"So somebody has to break the chain."

"That's exactly it. You're learning fast."

"So how do I deal with Wayno then?"

"You need to appear unaffected by him. Stay in control. It's best to not get annoyed because that is exactly what they want you to be."

"Then what if it carries on?"

"Tell an adult. They may be able to help you and protect others. Telling on a bully is actually a brave thing to do."

"And well worth it if it stops the same thing happening to

someone else," Jerry added with a smile. "But isn't it grassing?"

"Well, that's what the bully wants you to think. If someone broke into your house would you tell the police?"

"Of course."

"Isn't that grassing on the burglar?"

Jerry laughed.

Jerry felt lonely once back at school. None of his mates were playing football and Mindy could not be found in her usual haunts. In fact even Chloe wasn't sure where she hung around anymore.

"Haven't seen her for a few days," Chloe complained sulkily. "I thought she was my mate, but she's turned like well-moody." Her expression changed to one of sympathy. "Why? Has she dumped you already?"

Just then Jerry noticed a few other girls listening in on their conversation. Vikki's eyes lit up.

"God, what a tramp." She spun round delighted. "Oi, Tamsin, Mia – you gotta hear this."

After a quick confab one of the other girls squealed, "Ooh, she's so up herself. Thinks she's some sort of glamour model."

Jerry sighed and left the girls to it. That's all he needed: more gossip proving him to be a complete wimp and loser.

As he reached the mobile classes he became vaguely aware of a gang milling about by the bushes at the edge of the field and thought he recognised Silu and Rhino. But even with his new glasses on he couldn't trust his eyesight or powers of recognition.

Looking over to the gang by the bushes he could now see Matty and Silu together smoking and laughing with Rhino. Then he saw Miss Powys approaching.

"Good morning, Jerry."

"Hiya Miss."

She carried a bulging briefcase and a plastic carrier bag.

"Let me help you, Miss."

"Thank you." She looked relieved as he took both bags from her. The plastic bag contained red exercise books and Jerry was surprised by how heavy both loads were, making him feel a new respect for his form tutor. Miss Powys led the way up the ramp and got out a large bunch of keys. She stared at them for a few moments then selected one and was about to push it in the key hole with her other hand on the handle when she stopped.

"Oh." The door was already open. Jerry's immediate thought involved Wayno.

As they entered the small lobby Jerry's arms ached from carrying the bags but he knew he couldn't put them down yet. Miss Powys pushed open her classroom door, took one step in then stopped. Jerry bumped into her.

"Hello Stephen. How did you get in?"

Jerry plumped the bags on the teacher's desk and realised he had never been so pleased to see another fellow pupil.

"Hello Miss, hello Jerry," Stephen responded casually. "Oh, my Dad let me in. Hope you don't mind"

"Ah, of course. No that's fine, Stephen. Just don't tell the others."

Jerry looked confused. Miss Powys saw his puzzled expression and smiled.

"Stephen's dad is Frank, the caretaker."

"You mean Director of Maintenance and Security," the pupil corrected the teacher.

"Oh yes, sorry." Miss Powys aimed a humorous scowl at Jerry who grinned.

"So we're allowed to come here in the mornings then?" Jerry asked.

"Not officially, but Stephen has requested it as a safe haven and I told him he could sit quietly at break and lunchtimes doing homework or sometimes helping me with odd jobs."

"I could do with a safe haven right now," Jerry admitted.

"Yes, you and Stephen have quite a bit in common, Jerry.

Perhaps you should consider helping each other out. I'm happy for you to come here and help me sort stuff out, pin up displays, that sort of thing. If you promise to be friends with Stephen – that's the deal. Think of this place as sanctuary."

Jerry nodded whilst frowning in deep thought.

"You see, Stephen has been on the wrong side of Wayne too," Miss Powys added.

Jerry looked at his classmate with new eyes.

"Yeah and Rhino," Stephen admitted. "They call me a boff and laugh when I go to the library." Stephen spoke so nonchalantly that Jerry envied him, wishing he could keep so calm without letting it wind him up. Worse than the actual humiliation of being bullied were the sleepless nights of stress and fear. Being bullied became a feeling which stayed with you wherever you were, at any time.

"Sorry about the other day." He put out a hand, gratefully taken by Stephen. "I took my anger out on the wrong person."

"Yes, I understand. I used to take it out on my brother until I realised I was as bad as them."

Miss Powys, sorting out her books on her desk, looked up and smiled.

"It occurs to me that you two boys should work together. Help each other. Use this place as a bolt-hole – remember to keep it secret, though. I'm usually here at lunch and short breaks, so feel free to pop in and I might find you jobs to help me out too."

"Thanks Miss P." Jerry felt a new surge of confidence.

"That does mean you two will have to fend for yourselves at morning break, but it's only twenty minutes."

Jerry mused upon this new challenge.

"Do you play football, Stephen?"

"No. Can't stand the game. Don't see the point in kicking a bag of air around. No, I go to the library at break time to read the paper."

"Okay, we'll meet here at lunch then."

After a double period of History, Jerry used morning break time to look for Mindy. He decided to beg for her forgiveness and confess his pride and stupidity.

Just then he saw her at a distance, walking with a few friends, so he fell in behind her, unseen. To his surprise she waved to her friends and walked on alone across the front of school. Then his worst fears were quickly confirmed when he saw Wayno ambling towards her with a fag hanging from his thin lips. He removed the cigarette, blew a white tube of smoke to one side and then kissed her. That ugly yellow-toothed git was snogging his Mindy. What the hell was going on? It occurred to Jerry that what he hated most was his own jealousy and the realisation he should have done exactly what Wayno presently did – kiss Mindy when he had the chance. But it seemed his chance had slipped away now. Undeterred Jerry kept walking towards them.

Wayno spotted him approaching. Close up Jerry could see the obvious line of stitches on his top lip – his own handiwork – making the bully even more unsightly than usual.

Wayno slipped an arm over Mindy's shoulders and like a tentacle it wound around her neck pulling her closer to him. Jerry studied her expression and she seemed content with the situation.

"Come for a fight have you, four-eyes?" Wayno released Mindy and pulled his hands up in a defensive boxing pose. "Come on then – my chance to even things up."

"Leave it Wayne baby," said Mindy suddenly. She put her left hand behind Wayno's head and leaned in to kiss him again. Then she took his cigarette, pinching it between thumb and forefinger and held it confidently to her lips. She inhaled expertly, removed the cigarette and smiled at Jerry. He watched confused as wisps of smoke fluttered from her nostrils billowing into white clouds that formed a barrier between them.

At that moment Jerry became aware of his glasses slipping down his nose. Now he either had to peer over the top of the frames like an academic twit or push them back up with his finger thus only emphasising the existence of his spectacles, which he didn't want to do and would only cause further derision.

"It's okay, I don't fight people with glasses. See I respect disabilities and would never punch a spazzo."

When Mindy joined in with the uproarious laughter Jerry spun round and walked off ignoring the chicken noises and trying to block out the expletives hurled at him. He thought he heard Silu's voice in there somewhere too.

He blinked back tears wondering what had happened to the world. Could Mindy really be so fickle and shallow? Excitement and danger were clearly more attractive prospects. Being 'nice' just didn't cut it if you wanted someone like Mindy. At least he understood now.

The rest of the day passed without further incident. The more he thought about the earlier events the more it made him seethe. His walk home became a lonely dawdle. Wayno. What a bastard! What made him so great? He thinks he can treat people any way he wants to. What the hell Mindy saw in him was a mystery to Jerry. How he hated Wayno. He wished someone would rip his head off; or even better – torture him mercilessly for eternity until he screamed and begged for forgiveness. He wanted Wayno to know what it felt like to be beaten and made to feel low enough that you start to hate yourself. He also wished he had the powers to make Wayno short-sighted.

Before reaching his own street he fished his mobile phone from his bag, switched it on and after selecting 'suppress' he scrolled down to the school number then pressed 'call'. He got quickly through to the switchboard where a recorded voice listed a number of options - he ignored them all and held on to get through to a receptionist. Eventually he recognised the friendly tones of Mrs Billington.

Jerry frowned and put on a deep voice. "Hallo, yes. I'd like to register a complaint about a certain pupil from your school." Jerry gave a detailed and very accurate description of Wayno, including the stitches, until he was sure they must know who he meant. "This boy has been drinking alcohol and smoking in the little area behind your school with the trees at the edge of your field. I can see him from my window. In fact I have seen him taking drugs too – he leaves things behind that I believe is proof of drug-taking." Jerry halted unsure what the proof and paraphernalia were he would need to describe. "I live just round the corner and I'm forever getting things thrown in my garden – er ... cigarettes, cans, bottles and even, um, hypodermic syringe, needle-thingies, you know ..." He stopped, hoping he hadn't gone too far.

"Oh I see," Mrs Billington replied. "And your name is?"

"I'd prefer this to remain anonymous as I'm worried about being threatened by this lout. I'm sure you understand my predicament."

"Well would you like to talk to Mr Finn our Deputy Head?"

"No, no, I think I've said my piece, thank you," Jerry stumbled, sure that Quincy would recognise his voice immediately. "I hope you'll find some suitable way of punishing this little ... hooligan." He cringed at his poor improvisational skills, trying to remember what he'd learnt in Drama lessons. Pressing 'End call' Jerry closed his phone and slotted it in his trouser pocket.

That evening, once dark, Jerry slipped out of his front door unseen and took a few items from the recycling bin and put them in his bag.

Chapter Thirteen

When Jerry left half an hour earlier in the morning his mum took it as a sign that things were getting better. Jerry walked a different way to school, reaching the wooded area at the edge of the field before the usual mob got there. From his bag he took an empty bottle of vodka and two bent beer cans, which he threw behind a bush. The items had left a sludgy residue at the bottom of his bag which had stained his Maths book, but he felt it was worth the aggravation it might cause. Once done he walked around a few blocks until it seemed a good time to arrive at school. He waited for a big group of students, which he joined the back of so as to remain unnoticed, and was glad to see Wayno and Rhino in their usual place, making gestures at cars and passers-by.

Strolling to the mobile classroom he felt like whistling aloud, but managed to restrain himself. The door opened and he greeted Stephen with a smile. Stephen grunted and then went back to his thousand page book, which suited Jerry well. There was no need for silly pleasantries. Instead Jerry stood by the window where he could survey both the front of the school and much of the playing field. Almost like clockwork he saw Wayno and a little gang of cronies strut across the grass towards the bushes and wooded area for a smoke. As they disappeared into the trees the door opened as Miss Powys entered, puffing and hauling more heavy bags into the room.

"Miss, miss – I swear I just saw Wayno and Rhino in those bushes. They were smoking and drinking I swear Miss, I saw them."

"Woah. Good morning to you too, Jerry," the teacher said still dragging a heavy bag across the floor. "How about giving me a hand here?"

"Sorry, miss." Jerry jogged towards her and lifted the weight with some difficulty onto her desk. In his corner, Stephen looked up as if annoyed to be distracted again from his riveting read. "It's just that it'd be good to catch them, wouldn't it? In the act."

"Drinking you say?" Miss Powys looked thoughtful. "How can you be sure?"

"First it was beer and then it looked like something … you know … stronger."

"But did you see it? It might have just been fizzy or water."

"They were bragging about it, miss. Showing off – you know what Wayno's like. Can't keep his gob shut."

"Mm. Well, I should go and do something about it." Miss Powys began walking towards the door. "You both stay here."

Back at the window Jerry kept watch as Miss Powys talked on her phone whilst bustling determinedly across the football pitches. Just as he contemplated rushing out to help her he saw a wondrous sight. Mr Finn talking into his phone suddenly appeared streaking across towards the bushes at a terrific rate. Even though he began a good two hundred metres behind Miss Powys he quickly overtook her and surged into the little woods. Suddenly a handful of pupils appeared from nowhere, like magic, scattering and spilling across the field as the two teachers perpetrated a hilarious game of catch. Jerry hugged himself in delight.

Giving his glasses a quick polish, Jerry stared ahead not wanting to miss the best bit. Finn gave good chase and quickly got hold of Wayno who dangled limply in the man's fearsome grip. Meanwhile Miss Powys prodded about in the bushes completely disappearing for a while, until she stepped out again into the sunlight holding aloft her trophies: a bottle and a can. Jerry sniggered and punched the air.

"You've gotta come and see this mate." Jerry turned to share the moment with his new friend, but Stephen just grunted and turned his page over. "What do you think, Stevie?" Jerry smiled. "That Wayno deserves everything that's coming to him."

"Possibly," Stephen said with little interest. "I believe in karma – what goes around comes around."

"Yeah, but sometimes karma needs a bit of a helping hand," Jerry smiled, keeping an eye on the joyful scene.

"Well, I find that rarely works to be honest. Who are we to judge?" Stephen went back to his book. "And by the way, don't ever call me Stevie again or I'll call you Jeremy."

To Jerry's delight Mr Finn walked Wayno straight past the mobile. Having seen them coming in his direction, Jerry had opened the window and stood peeking surreptitiously through the gap. They walked almost exactly below him.

"So what nefarious deeds were going on behind the bushes then?"

"Nothing, sir."

"Well if you're not smoking or drinking then pray tell me what else you boys were doing cosily in the bushes together?"

"Are you saying I'm gay, sir?"

And their voices trailed away. Jerry would have paid good money to have heard the rest of the conversation. Surely now this would be the end of Wayno.

The tension mounted when Miss Powys didn't appear for registration. Instead it was taken by Miss Ngedi the strict cover supervisor who had them sat in silent rows until they filed out. It became unbearable when it got to lunchtime and there was still no word about the investigation and no sign of Miss Powys. Once he'd eaten his sandwiches in the mobile classroom he interrupted the quietly reading Stephen.

"I wonder if Wayno's been expelled yet?"

Stephen shrugged.

"I think this is the end of my problems."

"Let's hope so, Jerry. Then I'll get to finish my book."

Just as Jerry gave up hope of hearing any news today the door opened and in came Miss Powys sighing melodramatically. She walked wearily over to her desk and slumped on the chair.

"Goodness me. All this detective work has quite worn me out."

Jerry got up and sat on the desk in front of her. Even Stephen put his book down.

"Well, miss? Is he gone? Can we celebrate yet?"

Miss Powys looked up with a confused expression.

"Has Wayno been permanently excluded?" Jerry felt all his worries begin to drift off into the ether.

"Oh, I see. Um, no. It's a little more complicated than that."

The disappointment hit Jerry like being told shockingly bad news.

"But he brought alcohol onto the school premises. What's complicated about that?"

"Well we can't prove it was Wayne." Miss Powys replied.

"I saw him," Jerry snapped.

"Then it would be your word against his. You're the guy who sent him to hospital recently, Jerry." She shrugged. "Don't shoot the messenger."

Jerry checked his tone, knowing she was right. "Sorry miss. But you found the vodka bottle, right?"

"Yes but I didn't actually see him drinking it. There were other people there too. How did you know it was vodka?"

"Is Wayno still with Finn?"

"Mister Finn. Yes, but it's not just Wayne. We did a lot of detective work today and we think we've caught the whole gang. We trawled through hours of CCTV tape and got pictures of him and others smoking. We even got his girlfriend."

Jerry froze with horror.

"Oh and one of your friends seems to be involved. Sachindra is it? Silu. In fact he has told Mr Finn that the vodka bottle is his. It's hard for us to prove otherwise."

Jerry was stumped. Mindy? Silu too? This wasn't part of the plan. He had imagined seeing Wayno expelled and escorted off the premises by Quincy Finn OBE amidst the jeering and booing of the entire school, all amassed to watch the shaming of the hated bully. In his mind he also included a scene with Wayno in the stocks being pelted with rotten fruit as well as much harder and more lethal objects.

"But Mindy wasn't involved, miss," Jerry said hurriedly.

"Who?"

"Parminder Sidhu."

"I didn't say she was. How do you know anyway? You seem to know more about this than you're letting on." Miss Powys narrowed her eyes and looked him over.; "Is there something you want to tell me, Jerry?"

"Nor Silu, miss. I know for a fact that he doesn't drink alcohol. It's against his religion or something. His dad'd go berserk if he finds out," Jerry added in a panic.

"Then it's up to Silu to explain why he's saying what he is."

"He's being threatened."

Miss Powys turned away. "Well it's possible, but very difficult to prove. Anyway, the smoking thing has become a separate issue. There is a lot of film of Wayne and one particular girl smoking inside the front gates. If she's stupid enough to go out with someone like Wayne Cadman then she deserves all she gets."

It was a convincing argument but Jerry couldn't let Mindy suffer because of him. Having said that, there wasn't much he could do about the smoking issue – that was her choice and she had to live with the consequences. Silu on the other hand ...

When Miss Powys gave him another intense look Jerry felt himself redden.

"I saw Wayno and Rhino drinking beer too."

"Oh right."

"Did you find the cans?"

Miss Powys got up and sat on the edge of her desk facing Jerry. "No – just the bottle and a can of coke. You still haven't answered my question about how you knew it was vodka."

Dismissing the query Jerry tried to think clearly as he spoke to avoid contradicting himself.

"Those two had cans of beer and a bottle but I only saw those two drinking."

"Okay, but again it's only your word against theirs – we need proof. I want to kick those two out as much as you do but without hard evidence ..." Miss Powys looked wistful.

"You'll find the cans in the bushes near where the vodka bottle was," Jerry blurted out.

"Now how exactly do you know that?"

"I told you I saw them." Jerry's mind raced through all the logical permutations of this lie. The problem with lies was that they spawned innumerable new lies until you became entangled in your own trap.

"What, you were over by the bushes drinking with them?"

"No," Jerry mumbled. "They were threatening me."

"Was this on the field by the bushes? Why would you be so stupid as to go there?"

"No no, miss, we were by the front gate."

"What and Wayne was drinking by the front gate?"

"No – smoking."

"Yes, I've seen the CCTV footage of him and his girlfriend smoking and even talking to you, so that's true," the teacher murmured. "So they had the drinks then?"

"But I told you before, she wasn't involved at all. Mindy didn't threaten me and she wasn't drinking either," he added hurriedly.

"Right, but what about the alcohol? How do you know about it?"

Jerry began to lose the threads he'd been carefully weaving until now.

"He had it all in a bag. He was bragging about it."

Miss Powys stood up.

"Aha, so he was carrying a bag. So all we need to do is look at the security pictures again and if he's holding a bag and you can identify it then we've got him." She clenched a fist. "I think this is it, Jerry. Well done." She walked up to him and patted him on the shoulder. "You go and see Mr Finn now and tell him what you just told me. I'll go and investigate the bushes for more evidence."

At that moment Jerry's heart sank as he realised the impossibility of his situation. What an idiot. There was no way he could tell Mr Finn about the bag of beer without being caught out. The CCTV footage would show him to be a liar. He had to go and see Mr Finn but what exactly would he say?

"Sounds a bit fishy, Jerry," Stephen said with a puzzled expression.

Jerry rolled his eyes and breathed out heavily.

"You wouldn't believe me if I told you."

"Do the right thing, Jerry. It'll be best in the long run."

Jerry sneered, mocking the voice out loud.

"Yah, do the right thing, Jerry. I always do the bloody right thing. It seems to me you don't get anywhere in this world by 'doing the right thing' – by being decent or conventional. It's the bullies who get what they want in life by pushing us wimps around. I'm sick of being a goody-goody. Why can't Wayno just be kicked out for good so the rest of us can bloody well get on with our lives?"

"Keep focussed, Jerry," said Stephen ignoring Jerry's imploring speech. "Don't get yourself into trouble too. Wait for him to slip up – because he will in time."

He turned to begin his lonely walk to the office of Quincy Finn OBE. His knock was muffled and barely audible and just as he wondered whether he should knock again he heard a voice thunder through the woodwork.

"Come in."

Furtively Jerry pushed the door inwards and stood on the threshold to await his judgement.

"Ah, Jerry. Just the very man. You must be in the mind-reading business, young chap. I was just thinking I needed to see you."

"Oh," was all Jerry could manage in response.

"Now then, Miss Powys tells me you were the one to alert us with a tip-off regarding this whole ugly business. Would you be kind enough to tell me again, including as much detail as you can muster up please."

"I do have something to tell you, sir," he replied swiftly.

"Good good. The more evidence we can produce against these nasty thugs the quicker we can get them out and the better it will be for everyone."

For an instant Jerry considered changing his story again, but knew the lying had to stop.

"I planted the bottles in the bushes to get Wayno into trouble." Jerry felt himself being slowly crushed by the traumatically intense hush.

"Ah, I see." Mr Finn put his pen to his mouth and tapped a rhythm on his teeth. "Right."

"Parminder Sidhu and Silu – I mean Sachindra Patel – didn't do anything wrong. Please don't get them into trouble."

"Uh-huh." Mr Finn began to suck the top of his pen in contemplation.

"I know. It was stupid but I've had enough of being made to look like an idiot."

"I see."

"I'm really sorry for all the trouble I've caused."

"Mmm. I see." Mr Finn repeated calmly.

Jerry wished he would stop saying "I see" and just shout at him. He deserved as much. But somehow Mr Finn's quiet, collected demeanour became even more frightening than his full-on blustering, blasting mode.

The terrifyingly long silence seemed longer than an ice-age. Something was brewing in the Deputy-Head's mind and he knew he was about to receive the full brunt of the storm which would surely ensue.

"I accept any punishment you give me, sir. I won't argue or complain."

"Glad to hear it, young man," Mr Finn said without looking his way. Finally, he removed his pen from his mouth and spun on his chair towards Jerry.

"What you've done is incredibly stupid. You've certainly made Miss Powys and me look like idiots, so I hope you're not proud of what you've done."

Jerry shook his head solemnly.

"Your punishment is quite straight forward, Jerry." He left a long, dramatic pause as he turned back to his desk to jot down a few notes. Then he slowly turned to the boy and gave him a hard stare.

"Your punishment is this ... I'm going to make you a prefect."

Jerry looked up. "I don't understand, sir. A prefect?"

"Ye-es," said Mr Finn elongating the 'e'. "Now that might not sound like a punishment but with status comes great responsibility, expectations and commitment of time and energy. You will have to work very closely with Mr Platt. I want you to make a big effort to get on with him and become partners in a big project we are about to spearhead. Do you think you can cope with that?"

Jerry nodded dumbly still startled by this shock announcement.

"Unfortunately you have wasted my valuable time but I'm willing to overlook it and see the bigger picture here. If anything, Jerry, I'm a little disappointed not to have the evidence I need to kick out those damn hooligans, but c'est la vie. This world is full of blighters who spoil things for everyone else. They can't quite see things the way we do, eh?" To Jerry's amusement Mr Finn actually winked at him.

Just at that moment there came a knock at the door and it opened to reveal Miss Powys brandishing the newly-found beer cans.

"Bagsy I be Sherlock and you're Dr Watson," she said with a grin, which soon disappeared when the other two didn't respond as she expected. "Have I missed something?"

Mr Finn stood up and beckoned her in. She closed the door and sat next to Jerry.

"Afraid so." He raised his arms up in a stifled yawn and touched the ceiling without straightening his elbows. It reminded Jerry of the man's awesome presence both physically and in terms of charisma. "It seems this young gentleman took it upon himself to frame the miscreants in an attempt to devise a miscarriage of justice and go over our heads making us look like fools in the meanwhile."

"Is this true, Jerry?"

The lad closed his eyes and nodded.

"Oh Jerry!" Miss Powys' tone was unbearable. "I really expected better from you. So what do we do now?"

The worst bit for Jerry became the fact that he had disappointed two people he really respected. He didn't think his parents would be thrilled either.

"Well, that really depends on Jerry now," Mr Finn folded himself in half to sit down, his knees coming above the level of his desk. "To be fair to him he had the courage to admit the truth to me – which doesn't change the fact that presumably he lied to you."

"I'm sorry, miss, I really am. It won't happen again, I promise." He pressed his fingers into his eyes in embarrassment.

"In a skewed kind of way his motive was an admirable one and he certainly showed tremendous creativity and initiative. For that reason I have made him a prefect working alongside

Mr Platt on our new zero-tolerance bullying project. I'm sure this young man will be brimming with ideas — as long as they are legal and respectable."

Miss Powys nodded and pouted with approval.

"Thank you, sir. I promise not to let you down."

"Good, because I'm trusting you. I also see no need on this occasion to involve your parents, but I want you to understand that if anything like this happens again your record will look very poor and further drastic steps will be taken."

"Yes, sir."

"What do you think, Miss Powys?"

Jerry's form tutor pouted again. "Yes I think we can draw a line underneath this incident and move on in a positive way. But we expect results from you on this project, Jerry. You will be the students' spokesman on this — as a victim of bullying yourself. I want you to understand that this is a terrific responsibility for you to take on. We're trusting you on this one because we know you're a good lad with the right intentions." She looked to Mr Finn, deferring to his natural authority.

"Splendid. One of the things I like about you Jerry is your loyalty to your friends. You came here and told me the truth, which would have been too frightening a prospect for many pupils." He laughed a deep, dark chuckle, like a villain from an old horror film. "But friendship and the oath of trust overcame your fear. That's the reason I like you, Jerry. In the end you know it is best to do the right thing." Jerry looked up on hearing that phrase again. When Mr Finn stretched his legs out both he and Miss Powys automatically pulled their own legs further under their chairs to make room. "Catching these horrible hooligans is going to take someone brave and creative," Mr Finn continued. "I think you are just our man."

Chapter Fourteen

"Okay, so my idea turned out to be a crappy one. I admit it," Jerry said sullenly to Stephen next morning at school. "Let's see what you've got."

"It didn't work, Jerry, because it involved lying. Lies are never the answer."

"Feel free to say 'Yah, told you so'," said Jerry resignedly.

"Why would I want to do that? I take no pleasure in someone else's pain. I only want to help you."

"Okay then," Jerry said, sitting on the desk in front of Stephen. "I need to come up with a plan."

"Invite Wayno round to your house for a cup of tea."

"Do what?"

"Extend the hand of friendship," Stephen persisted. "It's by far the best way of dealing with enemies. It's called the element of surprise. Or if you prefer – a pre-emptive strike."

"Wow. That would certainly surprise Wayno," Jerry laughed whimsically.

"You might be amazed by the result – but you need to have balls of steel."

"Stranger things have happened," Jerry admitted. "After all, I became your friend and it doesn't get much stranger." Stephen tutted and rolled his eyes as if admonishing a child.

"So I get him to my house," Jerry said seriously. "What then?"

"Well that all depends on you Jerry."

"God, it's so annoying when you talk in riddles."

"How will you learn anything if I just tell you all the

answers?"

Jerry pulled a face.

"God, it's even more annoying when you're right."

"I've been doing some detective work for you, Jerry, and I have something very interesting to tell you about Wayne Cadman…"

This gave him a day to sort out his plan which he would put into practice tomorrow.

At home, without his parents suspecting anything, Jerry carefully planned out all the details and checked his resources. That night he slept well.

"Bloody hell four-eyes, you really don't learn do you?"

The pack bayed with laughter as Wayno stood by the school gates shaking his head leering at Jerry.

"Which part of your face shall I smash to smithereens first?"

Jerry stared straight back at him trying not to blink.

"You better choose quickly because the camera's waiting for you," Jerry stuck his thumb over his shoulder as coolly as he dared.

No one spoke or laughed this time as everyone stood still creating what would probably make an excellent tableau on the CCTV film in the camera pointing directly at the front gates of the school.

"Just delaying the inevitable, goggles. Another time, another place," Wayno put on his best gangster voice.

"How about my house at 4.30?" Jerry blinked quickly a few times and then fixed his stare again.

"What to have a teddy bears' picnic with your cuddly toys and mummikins?"

"No. Just you and me."

"What is this a date? Are you asking me out?" Wayno put one hand on his hip and dangled the other with a limp wrist whilst swinging round to get a reaction from his cronies. Jerry couldn't see Silu but he spotted Matty hanging around near the back of the crowd. Some chuckling began.

"Why? Are you scared?" Jerry managed this line without a hint of a tremble.

It got a big reaction from the crowd. "Oo-oooh!"

No way could Wayno ignore Jerry now.

"Scared? Give me your address, you four-eyed freak, and I'll be there at 4-30."

That gave Jerry about half an hour to get home and set things up. With nobody home he was free to move the ladder in the garden into the appropriate position and do a final test before attempting the real thing.

At 4.33 Jerry opened the door to Wayno. Outside he saw a group of half a dozen people walk away. Amongst them was Mindy who Jerry saw looking back. He felt a thrill of fear mixed with the excitement of danger. It felt like he'd taken a dose of extra strong caffeine. There was no way of knowing how this would pan out.

"Brought your gang then?" Jerry said with a nervous smile.

"They're going. I'm on my own now. Just you and me."

Jerry said nothing but held his composure which took a great deal of effort.

"One thing I have to say about you, four-eyes, is you got balls," Wayno growled in a Clint Eastwood-type drawl.

Jerry buzzed with the thrill of the adrenalin rush. It was a kind of compliment – in fact the nicest thing Wayno had ever said to him.

"Why don't you come in?" He held open the door and gestured inside.

Wayno stayed on the threshold craning his neck round to try and see inside.

"Is this some kind of trap? You got Mr Finn and all your teacher buddies in there?"

"No-one. I'm the only person here," he replied. "Would you

like a cup of tea?"

"Nah, you can't get pissed on that." He strutted past Jerry and went into the living room, checking everything out as if casing the joint. "Got any booze, man? Or do you only buy alcohol when you're framing somebody?"

So he knew about that. Finn obviously had spoken to the bully and then been forced to apologise.

"You know," Wayno said as he admired the plasma television, "that stunt you pulled wasn't very nice. I think you need to apologise."

This wasn't quite how he'd planned the visit. Somehow he'd naively expected Wayno to be more compliant.

"You know what? You're right." Jerry tried to remember all the advice he'd been given so far. "It was a stupid thing to do and I am genuinely sorry. I wasn't thinking straight when I did it. I've told Mr Finn it was me and that I regret my stupid actions."

Wayno appeared taken aback by this. "Hope you get punished then. Otherwise that ain't fair."

"I've got to spend lunchtimes and after school with Mr Platt for the next few weeks," Jerry explained truthfully.

Wayno smirked and let out a whispery hiss just like a snake might make if it laughed. "Old Pratty. What a complete joke he is. Not exactly a scary punishment – what's he going to do? Bore you to death?"

As the two boys laughed together Jerry wondered what on earth was going on. It seemed to be going too well but he stayed on guard for any unpredictable turn, which was just as well, because Wayno looked equally uncomfortable.

"Look here goggles. I'm not your mate, you know. I haven't forgotten what you did to me. In fact if it wasn't for that Paki bitch I'd have ripped out your spinal column by now."

That insult hurt Jerry like a stab wound.

"Don't talk about Mindy like that."

"Oh yeah, I forgot – she was your bird wasn't she? Then she

dumped you for me. Says you didn't even kiss her. That you're a bit of a nancy-boy. When she came to me I was in the mood just then for a bit of extra spice. Know what I mean? Nah, you probably don't."

Jerry's head swirled. The thought of Wayno touching his Mindy and those two together filled him with seething anger.

"She's the school bike. Every boy in the school except you has ridden that slag. She came to me 'cos she wanted a real man."

Through his glasses he could hardly see at all. Hatred made Jerry's sight all misty and shaken.

"You take those comments back about Mindy."

"Who?" Wayno's eyes narrowed above his twisted, gurning mouth. "What the Paki bitch? Oh is that her name? I wouldn't know – we don't do a great deal of talking – you know what I mean? Actions speak louder than words, eh?"

Jerry stood incredulous with no idea what to do now. If he punched Wayno he would be murdered in cold blood. He imagined Stephen's voice saying, 'Stay calm, Jerry. He's not worth it.'

Jerry grinned and shook his head slowly.

"Let's make this fair shall we?" he said.

"Huh?"

"I take my glasses off and you remove your contact lenses."

Discomfort registered itself immediately in Wayno's face in the form of a slight twitch.

"How d'you know that?"

"I know more than you think. You see we have quite a lot in common, you and me."

"I ain't no four-eyed freak like you."

"Oh," Jerry replied whilst pulling a face. "Then tell me what that writing says on the side of that bag next to the shed ... without your contacts." He pointed out the window. "You can't can you? Nor can I if I take my glasses off. So let's make this fair."

Jerry made a big mime of taking off his glasses and putting them in their case and placing them on the table. "Or are you scared?"

Wayno stared dumbly, stunned with his mouth wide-open, catching flies.

Jerry felt the adrenalin pumping through every vein and corpuscle. The usual mist and swirl occurred before him but, somehow, it gave him strength. He was the Knight of Myopia.

It worked. Wayno took out a small plastic container, fished out his lenses with his little finger, which he deposited carefully in the container, then replaced it into his pocket. Wayno looked less confident now.

"Do you know what? I'm not in the least bit scared of you," Jerry continued. "I actually feel sorry for you. Thank God I'm not like you. And you call me a freak?"

Wayno's lips began to quiver as an energy began to stir inside him. One side of his face tightened, moving swiftly down both arms to his fingers that flexed with a tingling sensation. Then it affected his legs which bent into a springing position after which he leapt from his feet towards Jerry.

Expecting to feel a sharp pain Jerry jerked his body to one side only to watch Wayno shoot past uncontrollably into the sofa. Wayno got up and swung his head around confused and angry before crouching in some kind of martial arts pose. Jerry made for the back door.

"Oi, Cadman," Jerry called with some nerve. "Out here." Scrambling with the key he got the door open and as calmly as he could he stepped outside and stood visibly in the middle of the lawn, bracing himself. His back garden sat snugly surrounded by a tall evergreen hedge and backed onto a little copse which gave them a great deal of privacy from any prying neighbours.

"You little git. I'm gonna rip your head off ..."

"Yeah, yeah," Jerry said in a bored tone. "You said that before. Didn't happen though did it?"

For once Wayno looked a little taken-aback – probably not used to his victims standing up for themselves, thought Jerry.

"Not so tough now, eh?" Jerry taunted, quickly checking everything was in position.

This caused another charge.

Jerry's pulse raced to dangerous levels, but in that split-second he felt a warm hazy mist around him and then relaxed into its embracing grip.

What happened next amazed Jerry considerably. He laughed as he watched Wayno leap at him in slow motion. Now only a few inches away from each other Jerry could study the boy's angry demeanour in some detail. First he saw bloodshot eyes with black bags above pock-marked, sunken cheeks. The mouth which was always twisted down now opened in a scowl; spittle gathering in the thin corners of his pale lips.

With some amusement Jerry watched as Wayno pulled back a fist, knuckles white with intensity. The fist then began its slow journey towards his own face and Jerry felt confident enough to wait until it came within a few inches before he calmly leaned to one side and watched the fist waft uselessly past him. The momentum of the failed punch was enough to cause Wayno to lose his balance. The boy stumbled forwards, his legs tangling with Jerry's. But as he looked on, Wayno slowly spread his arms and Jerry worked out that Wayno was attempting to grab his legs. Instead Jerry stepped out of the looping arms before they could enclose him and he watched the bully hit his head on a piece of crazy paving. The whole incident came as a shock to Jerry, but it made him feel powerful – like an invincible warrior.

Suddenly everything returned to normal speed as Wayno lay in a crumpled heap, holding his back in agony. Jerry almost felt sorry for him and felt willing to shake hands and let him go. It seemed the bully had other plans.

Standing up, Wayno rolled his head round a few times, his neck cracking at various intervals. He rotated both shoulders which also made gristly noises and with eyes almost popping from his head faced the enemy once more.

"I'm gonna kill ya!"

Jerry smiled. Now was the time for his plan to come into action. He hoped he'd wound up Wayno enough for this to work.

Jerry scrambled up the ladder, positioned to take him onto his roof. Once on the red slates he took a breath and waited for Wayno's next move.

Jerry became aware of a much cooler breeze with no shelter at this height. Wayno looked up and gripped the bottom of the ladder.

"Come and get me you short-sighted fairy!" How Jerry enjoyed saying that line!

With an expression of uncertainty Wayno began a slow ascent, gripping the ladder tightly and keeping his body close to the metallic rings.

Eventually Wayno got to the top and Jerry could see fear in his face. The boy refused to move his head which remained fixed ahead, with eyes bulging and streaming.

"Come and get me Cadman," Jerry hissed. "Unless you're too scared."

Wayno shook himself and made the final push over the top of the ladder and onto the sloping red slates of the house roof towards his quarry. Jerry had to remain guarded and in control now.

Shuffling slowly up towards him, Wayno slipped slightly and without a thought landed on his backside and froze in a seated position.

"I gotta get down," Wayno whimpered. "Need to get down. Please help me."

"The chimney's right behind you," Jerry suggested amicably. "Shuffle up on your bum, but mind any loose slates or you'll fall to your death." Jerry had to suppress a snort of laughter as he said this.

Painfully slowly, Wayno inched his way backwards up towards the chimney, holding out one hand which, finally, wrapped itself gratefully around the squared corners. Wayno gasped with relief as he hauled himself behind the chimney stack, with his back against the black and orange brickwork. His breathing became shallow and hoarse.

"Not so big and scary now are you?"

Wayno concentrated on his breathing, gulping noisily and hugging himself.

"I thought you were going to rip my head off or something. It's an incredible view," he continued. "Come over here and have a look."

Wayno shook his head and continued hugging his knees.

"Oh no, I've just remembered – you're short-sighted. You can't see all that way, can you?"

Jerry stepped carefully towards him.

"Would you like me to help you get down?"

Wayno looked up with the face of a little child and nodded helplessly.

This was an opportunity for some kind of negotiation, so Jerry thought hard about his next words.

"Do you promise to leave me and my friends alone now?"

Wayno nodded his head vigorously, pressing himself so fervently back into the chimney that it wouldn't have surprised Jerry if he turned into one of those stone gargoyles the same colour as the bricks. His facial expression was grotesque enough. It was then Jerry heard Wayno stammering – in genuine fear. He'd found the bully's weakness.

He almost felt sorry for Wayno now and put the final part of his plan into action.

"Take my hand and I'll get you down safely."

Wayno blubbered something inaudible.

"Oh for God's sake, don't be such a baby or else I'll tell everyone at school that you're scared of heights. Look I want you off my roof and if you want the same then you'll have to trust me."

Eventually he took Jerry's hand and slowly shuffled along the very top ridge of the roof on all fours.

"Stand up Wayne."

"I c-c-can't."

"Stand up now," Jerry commanded in his best impression of Finn.

Wayno closed his eyes and rose up carefully until he stood straight. He put both arms on Jerry's shoulder as if in affectionate embrace.

"Open your eyes." Jerry waited until his order was obeyed. "I promise you we'll both get down safely if you do as I tell you."

Smiling nonchalantly, Jerry enjoyed the moment when he finally had power over this boy who'd caused him so much stress and grief for so long. The change in status felt good. Wayno's arm began to tighten around his neck and throat.

"Any chance of you letting go? Look I'm really flattered but I don't feel the same about you."

But Wayno neither laughed nor let go.

Now for the dangerous bit, thought Jerry. With Wayno wrapped around him, eyes closed again, Jerry could just reach the rope and harness attached to their giant oak tree. The rope had been there all along in view, but Wayno had not seen it. In a well-practiced move Jerry pulled the rope tight and carefully attached it to the harness on his belt. He tested how secure it felt and remembered the exhilaration of the few practice-runs he had attempted before this moment.

"No sudden movements, Wayne." Jerry sidestepped then grabbed hold of the boy with all his might. He had to get this right. Looking down towards the lawn Jerry could see a swirling mesh and a hazy mist before him.

"Hold on tight!" he called into Wayno's ear. "We're going down!"

Wayno turned to look at Jerry and his face streamed with

119

tears – confused and pitiful. Jerry crouched, took a few quick steps and then flung himself and his passenger off the sloping tiles. Wayno shrieked like a banshee, kicking his feet against Jerry's shins whilst his arms swung wildly like broken windmills.

"Help me! Oh God, no. I don't want to die!" Wayno screamed in a high pitch squeal.

The two boys tipped with a jerking frenzy over the guttering and plummeted towards the back garden with a terrific velocity - rushing towards the garden. Then within inches of smashing into the floor they came to a sudden halt and just floated there upside down. Wayno now wheezing for breath in an asthma attack, went limp in Jerry's arms. Jerry dropped Wayno the last few feet. His nemesis lay on the grass below him, either unconscious or paralysed with fear.

After a few minutes Wayno shook his head clear, looked up at Jerry magically floating above him, glanced around for a point of escape; noticed the back door still open and scarpered through it, into the hallway and out of the front door.

Jerry released his harness and did a commando roll onto the lawn.

He lay on the grass for a long time; exhilarated and terrified. Before his parents returned he had to put away the ladder and return his dad's climbing harness to the shed.

Once inside and after a chance to get back his breath, Jerry attempted to still the images racing through his mind, and could only wish that now life might start going back to normal again.

Chapter Fifteen

Jerry enjoyed a quiet week at school. He wasn't particularly aware of Wayno or Rhino, but then again neither did he see Mindy, Silu or Matty. Each lunchtime spent with Mr Platt initially felt awkward as they mostly sat in silence. But Mr Platt did explain the big project which involved raising awareness of bullying and implementing as many tactics and methods of prevention and intervention as possible.

"The school council are also working on this, but it seems Mr Finn was very keen for you and I to work together. He assured me you would be full of creative, innovative ideas," Mr Platt explained.

Indeed, Jerry had been thinking about this a great deal recently. He also thought about his new friendship with Stephen. "One thing that did occur to me was that we could start a 'Buddy' system where anybody who felt alone or scared could be teamed up with someone else. I was thinking there might be some younger kids who are scared of walking about the school. I'd be happy to do this. At the end of each of my lessons, I would go and collect my 'buddies' from their classes where the teacher is waiting with them, and we could walk about at break or lunchtime as a group, going round and collecting people as we go."

Mr Platt nodded with pursed lips. "Sounds an eminently sensible idea, so far. Go on."

"So in a larger group we could look after each other better."

"When you say 'look after' this doesn't involve violence does it," Platty asked nervously.

"I'm not suggesting we become vigilantes, no. I believe in non-violence. The idea would be to avoid conflict by being a gang."

"I don't like the word 'gang'. That suggests trouble – youths with hoodies, knives – that sort of thing."

"Okay, I don't mean a gang, just that we'd be protected by the numbers. Bullies are not likely to come and pick on someone surrounded by half a dozen friends are they?"

"I suppose not."

"And you and Mr Finn could lead assemblies about zero-tolerance for bullying," Jerry continued feeling inspired now. "I think we should write to parents, Governors, local papers – even our MP."

"Yes, yes. All good ideas. We should certainly pull together as a school from the Governors right down to the year 7s. If the school are going to do this then it should be done properly and in style." Mr Platt became animated for the first time in Jerry's experience. "I think the letters should come from you, the pupils, but I'm very happy to help you write those and get them sent off."

"That's the spirit, sir," said Jerry with a kind smile. He held a hand up for a high-five which caused Mr Platt to look perplexed. The Head of Year lifted his own hand and placed it over Jerry's and shook it uncertainly.

Indeed letters were written, checked, redrafted and dispatched. They also wrote to local councils, the police, the Prime Minister, the BBC and every bullying support group and charity they could think of.

The buddying system began straight away with tutors recommending pupils requiring a buddy. There was an email address set up on the school website for victims to report bullying to Mr Platt and to apply to join the buddy system.

Rather than just have groups of pupils wandering aimlessly around school, Mr Finn set up an area in the hall where people selected by the teachers, mainly victims of bullying, were free to try out different activities such as drama, painting, chess, creative writing, photography, even an area for playing with games consoles was permitted. It became a chance for 'taster sessions' for already existing clubs. The system became such a success that within a week a third of the entire school had applied to join in, which wasn't practical, but it made the Head Leadership Team and Governors take a very active interest in what was going on.

All the school clubs increased in attendance which meant having fewer pupils roaming aimlessly at lunchtime, giving the staff on duty less stress. The buddy system worked very well with no individuals left alone to be picked on. The most surprising thing of all was how many people volunteered to help out. Lots of older pupils took on the responsibility of mentoring, helping and accompanying younger students, which had a very immediate effect on a number of previously unhappy, unmotivated and even schoolphobic pupils.

With the first initiative given the thumbs up, the think-tank which originally consisted of Jerry and Mr Platt, grew in size to include Mr Finn, Miss Powys, Stephen and two voluntary representatives from all the other years.

"How about this then," Jerry suggested to the meeting after the first successful week. "We focus on some of the types of bullying that occur. There are the obvious ones like racism, ageism and sizeism. We need to raise awareness that being different is absolutely fine. People are different shapes and sizes. They speak different languages and have accents. Some people are studious and others are sporty. We need to spread the word that if you love reading and want to be a librarian then that is fine and it doesn't make you a sad geek."

"Amen to that, brother," said Stephen with a smile, supported by a slow nod from Mr Platt.

"You're talking good sense so far, Jerry," Mr Finn said supportively. "How do you think we should go about raising awareness?"

"Well I can tell you my idea and maybe others can adapt my idea for their own purpose. You'll see what I mean if I explain it to you." Jerry had centre-stage and he collected his thoughts for his big moment. "You see, I get called four-eyes because I wear glasses and I know being short-sighted isn't a major disability – in fact being myopic has a few slight advantages. Anyway, having to wear glasses has always made me stand out." He stopped briefly and saw that everyone was intently listening.

"So my idea was this. To raise awareness for people who have bad eyesight and have to wear glasses I thought we could have a special day when everyone came to school wearing glasses, specs, shades - whatever. You know a bit like non-uniform day, except everyone wears uniform but has to have glasses of some kind. It's supposed to be fun and we could charge everyone a pound and the money could go to a blind charity. What do you all think?"

Jerry sat back in his chair and waited for a response. At first no-one spoke and Jerry wished he hadn't bothered saying anything

"That's brilliant, Jerry," Mr Finn exclaimed loudly. His support was quickly followed by nods, murmurs and superlatives. "Yeah. Excellent plan. Like it. Sounds cool."

"I know," Mr Platt said with a giggle. "We could call it 'Specs to School Day'."

More nods and positive mumblings showed the idea was agreed upon. One of the year 11 pupils immediately began to scribble on a piece of paper.

"We should create some sort of logo," he suggested as he scribbled quickly. "Something like this."

With a flourish he put the finishing touches to his lightning sketch and held it up. It said 'SPEX 2 SKOOL' in urban graffiti-type writing and the double 'o' in skool was turned into a pair of glasses with eyeballs peering through them.

"Um, perhaps we need to consider the spelling..." Mr Platt

began.

"No, no, it's wonderful," Mr Finn beamed, waving a hand at Mr Platt, which became a finger as if to admonish him. Mr Platt crossed his arms and sulked. "It's got to appeal to everyone. I think we should run with this idea. It needs a lot of organisation – we shouldn't rush into things – but who here agrees that we should go ahead with Jerry's idea and have a specs to school day?"

Jerry looked around, proud to see every arm raised, even Mr Platt's.

"Well, that's agreed then. I will propose the idea to the Head Leadership Team and Governors and I have no doubt that they will support me on this one. I shall certainly see to that. Right, meeting adjourned."

Everyone got up in unison and scraped back their chairs.

"That idea is wicked, eh sir?" one year seven pupil said directly to Mr Platt.

"Yes, absolutely," he replied.

"Yeah, well sick innit?"

Mr Platt looked around uncertainly. "Um, is it?"

The next few weeks sped by with all the planning and organisation. Jerry forgot about Wayno and Mindy. His head clamoured with ideas and plans. However, all this creativity was also becoming a distraction – as he discovered in his Maths lesson.

"Jerry? What answer would you give to this conundrum?"

His face fell when he realised he hadn't been listening to his teacher and now Old Haddock was using his low-level shouting voice: the one known as the calm before the storm.

"Sorry, sir, I don't know."

"Well work it out then you idiot. I've just spent the last ten minutes telling you how to use the formula."

"I ... I don't understand it sir." Jerry felt stupid in front of all the others.

After another hush Jerry waited for the volume to rise in Haydock's voice.

"I asked about five minutes ago if everyone understood. I said to put your hand up if you didn't. WHAT EXACTLY WERE YOU DOING, SONNY?"

Even though Jerry expected it the change in volume made him jump. What made it worse was that Old Haddock had a good point. Jerry had been day-dreaming and now looked very stupid in front of everyone.

"WELL? WHAT HAVE YOU GOT SAY FOR YOURSELF?"

This question sounded impossible to answer properly and Jerry wondered if Haydock meant it to be rhetorical or not. He focussed his mind back to the classroom and the snarling teacher noticing twenty five faces all turned round to face him.

"I'm sorry, sir. I was daydreaming and not listening to you. I don't know the answer."

Old Haddock was a little taken aback. "I see. WELL WHAT ARE YOU GOING TO DO ABOUT IT THEN?"

After a pause for thought Jerry looked the teacher in the eye.

"I'll make up the lost time by coming back here at lunch. Would you be willing to go through it again with me, sir if I promise to listen?" Jerry wondered which way Haydock would go.

"YES, YES, THAT'S FINE. NOW I SUGGEST THAT EVERYONE LISTENS TO ME NOW WITHOUT DAYDREAMING OR STARING OUT THE WINDOW." The volume lowered slightly to a stern yell. "Now then let's get through this lesson without any more silliness."

To Jerry's relief Old Haddock went through the formula again and Jerry concentrated this time and picked it up quite quickly, completing all the questions correctly before the end of the lesson. Once the bell went and everyone began disappearing Jerry took his book up to the front.

"Do you still want me to come back at lunch, sir?"

"Have you completed all the sums, boy?" Haydock still spoke far too loudly considering Jerry stood about two feet away from him.

Old Haddock flicked through his book, chewing his top lip. "You seem to have redeemed yourself somewhat young man. If you complete your homework and show all your working out we'll call it quits. You understand?"

Jerry nodded.

"BUT IF YOUR HOMEWORK'S NOT PERFECTLY CORRECT THEN YOU'LL HAVE A WEEK OF DETENTIONS. GOT IT?"

Jerry smiled benignly. "Yes sir. Thank you sir." He guessed that Old Haddock didn't really want to give up his precious lunchtime if he felt he'd got his message across another way.

"None of this silly business again, do you hear? Now off with you."

Jerry scampered off to meet his 'buddies' who would be waiting for him in the lunch room.

Jerry liked the fact that they looked up to him and that they considered him a hero. Even though they appeared to be a bunch of oddballs, he couldn't help warming to them. As he sat amongst them he smiled to hear their chattering and excitement as they told him about their various activities and achievements.

Something touched his shoulder and stayed there. Jerry looked round and saw some brightly painted fingernails.

"You're really good with the youngsters aren't you?" Jerry turned and looked up to see Mindy's smiling face. She stood alone and looked very serious. Her eyes no longer shone with their ever-constant smile. In fact her whole face seemed less animated and more forlorn. "I've been hearing all about your exploits."

"Yeah, I've heard about some of yours too," Jerry said, turning back to his lunch.

127

"What does that mean?" Mindy's voice sounded genuinely hurt. Jerry couldn't believe how insensitive she could be.

"Just leave me alone. You've made your choice."

"I was hoping we could talk." She pulled over a chair and sat next to him. All the year seven and eights nearby watched on in silence. Jerry hoped to keep his dignity.

"I've nothing to say. Why don't you tell your Dad what you've been up to."

"Why are you being like this?"

One of the year eight boys spoke up. "Is there any way we can help you Jerry?"

"It's okay, folk. We're finished here. Mindy was just leaving."

Mindy looked around and realised they had an audience. She gave Jerry a look of exasperation and left.

"Way to go, Jerry. That was cool."

"You sure told her, eh?"

But Jerry wasn't quite so sure.

Chapter Sixteen

A second unexpected thing happened that day.

Jerry arrived at the hall as usual to see which session was running. A year 11 student was leading an aerobics workout with boys and girls involved. Then he noticed Mr Finn seemed to be waiting for him in the corner. As the lunch club ran itself now without his input he walked up to the Deputy Head who leaned towards him confidentially.

"Follow me, Jerry." With a flick of the head he led the way back out of the studio and on a mazy walk to his own office, like the pied piper leading a child on a merry dance. Although bemused, Jerry followed obediently, assured by Quincy's manner and tone that he wasn't in trouble. Mr Finn opened his office door and entered and it wasn't until Jerry had closed the door and stepped in that he realised they possessed even less space than usual because of the presence of another person: Matty.

When Jerry took a second look at his old friend he saw cuts and bruises on his face. It clearly looked like he'd been crying too as he had tell-tale smudges and dirt across his cheeks under bloodshot eyes.

"Now then, I am led to understand that young Matthew here is a friend of yours, Jerry, so I hoped you'd be able to get some sense out of him."

Jerry nodded and sat next to Matty.

"You okay, mate? What happened?"

"Fell over."

"Come off it. You don't get a shiner like that from falling

over," Jerry smiled kindly. "Come on, I'm your friend – remember? I'm sure Mr Finn won't tell you off or shout if you just tell us the truth. Isn't that right, sir?" He knew this might be taking a liberty but it seemed worth a shot.

"We're here to protect you, so if you tell us who did this we can make sure it never happens again. You'll be safe and I promise you'll not be in trouble."

"It was just a fight that's all. I gave as good as I got."

"Is the other person in this school?" Jerry asked in his softest voice.

"No. It was outside of school. I got mugged." Matty sniffed and rubbed his eyes.

"Mugged?" Mr Finn said. "Then this is a police issue. I'll call them immediately and you can give them evidence. Perhaps we should take some photos."

"No!" Matty cried in an urgent tone. "No police. I'm fine. It's not important."

"But whoever did this needs to be dealt with," Jerry implored. "Just look at you."

"What's it gotta do with you?"

Mr Finn stood up – an imposing figure against the slouching snivelling scarecrow.

"Your friend here is concerned about you." He spoke in a firm but friendly manner. "Now I suggest you speak to him and tell him the truth. I know for a fact that Jerry is someone you can absolutely trust and he will do what's right. If Wayne Cadman had anything to do with this then it's essential you tell us."

"Wayno had nothing to do with this. It wasn't him. He didn't touch me," Matty blurted unconvincingly.

"Well then, perhaps it was done at home," Mr Finn suggested, giving Jerry a wink. "It's my duty to call in social services if I suspect one of my students is being beaten or abused at home..."

"No, please, don't get my parents involved," he broke down.

"Well, isn't it going to be rather difficult hiding this from your parents?" he asked perplexed. "I think they might notice the cuts on your face."

"I'll think of something," Matty mumbled with a pout.

"So what is it to be? Talk to Jerry or call in the police to investigate a case of GBH?" Finn said sternly. Behind his back, unseen by Matty he stuck up a thumb for Jerry to see. Jerry found it hard not to smile. The teacher's tactics were effective if a little extreme. "If I leave you two alone will you promise to tell him what really happened?"

Matty sniffed, wiped his nose on his sleeve, smudging the tears even more, and then nodded grudgingly. Quentin Finn OBE did the decent thing and left them to it.

"Come on Matty. I'm not an idiot," Jerry scolded, deciding to go for the tough no-nonsense approach. "It's pretty obvious Wayno bashed you up a bit. You're not scared of that moron are you?"

Matty merely stared at Jerry with an unpleasant look in his eyes.

"He deserves everything coming to him," Jerry continued. "Just tell old Quincy the truth and we'll be shot of Wayno forever. You don't need to fear him anymore."

At last Matty opened his mouth and took a deep breath. "He seems worried about you, though. What the hell did you do to him?"

Jerry felt his heart leap with the thrill of hearing that he had got one over on Wayno: got him 'worried'. How great that sounded. But seeing the state of Matty now made him realise the price of it.

"I don't think he'll be a problem anymore, Matty, my boy." Jerry nodded smugly and grinned at his own reflection in the window.

"No, that's where you're wrong, Jerry," Matty replied with a serious expression. "This was just a warning."

"What the hell do you mean?" Jerry asked with some

urgency. "What can he do? All we have to do is dob him in and it's over."

"Don't be so thick, Jerry. You're being a bit thick if you think it's that simple. Nothing's simple with Wayno. Everyone's better off if you just leave it as it is."

"What? Is it Mindy?" It began to dawn on Jerry that this wasn't really the end at all. "Are the rumours true?"

Matty shrugged. To Jerry this seemed like a confirmation. Wouldn't he have said if things were otherwise? Jerry felt a churning return to his stomach.

"And if you consider Silu to be a mate then don't say anything to Quincy or any of the teachers." Matty garbled as if he'd learnt a message by rote.

"What about Silu? Is this some kind of threat?"

"If you don't want to see Mindy or Silu hurt then back off now." Matty seemed uncomfortable as he spoke. "Don't be a supergrass, Jerry. Stop being teacher's nark and Wayno will back off."

"Why? What's happened? Tell me, Matty. Has something happened?"

"You're not listening to me." Matty looked away and rubbed a finger gently over one of the cuts on his cheek.

Jerry held two hands up in the air. "Okay, okay, I'm listening."

"Don't do anything silly. Please. We'll be okay if you keep your distance. Will you do that for us? Do it for Mindy."

"Why should I do anything for her?"

"Please, Jerry? Promise."

Against his better judgement he nodded and opened the door to signify the conversation was over to Mr Finn. The imposing man stooped back into his own office and looked hopefully to Jerry who shook his head with his nose wrinkled in disappointment.

The response from the community turned out better than

any of them could have imagined. The Governors wrote back to Jerry and the committee in full support of all the recommendations and agreed that "tackling bullying is to become one of our top priorities this academic year. If funding, resources or any kind of intervention or pre-emptive training is required then do not hesitate to contact us as monies are available for these important initiatives." The letter wished them luck in their endeavours.

The police were extremely helpful suggesting they send in community officers as the school saw fit to talk about the effects of bullying. The feeling of the committee was that police should be brought in as a deterrent and to make bullies realise the full seriousness and consequences of their actions.

Some parents had responded enthusiastically and said they would like to help out in some way. A few even gave times when they were free to come and lend a hand in person.

"Has anybody got any suggestions as to what we could get these people to do?" Mr Finn asked the group.

Jerry put up his hand. "I have. How about asking if they'd be willing to patrol the corridors at break and lunchtime? That's where most of the trouble happens. We could identify bullying hot spots and get adults and parents to walk about in groups. I know teachers are also on duty, but there are never enough of them to cover all the different places."

"Yes, that's good. I really like that. Our poor old teachers are too busy to do everything and asking over-worked, underpaid staff to police corridors I always think is an imposition." Quincy Finn pondered deeply. "Yes, I'll write back to them and propose the idea to see what the response is."

As the day wore on Jerry did his best to find Silu and Mindy but when he asked around it seemed that neither was at school. He tried Silu's mobile but each time only received a voice message telling him the phone was unavailable.

At lunchtime he waited at the front for Wayno who never

appeared. It seemed it might take a bit longer than assumed.

On the way home Jerry took a detour which took him to Mindy's house. The door was opened by Mindy's dad.

"Oh, hello Jerry. Haven't seen you for a while. How are you?"

"Fine thanks, Mr Sidhu."

"Come in." He stepped to one side to let him pass.

Mr Sidhu stopped him in the hallway and spoke in a serious voice.

"Is Parminder okay? We're very worried about her. She's been acting very strangely over the last few weeks and she won't talk to us." Mr Sidhu gave a pained expression. "I'm hoping you might know something."

"Well, that's partly why I came round," Jerry said with a look of sympathy. "I wanted to see if she's okay."

"Well, go through. She'll be glad to see you."

Jerry stepped into the front room as directed by Mrs Patel and he managed to stay calm considering what confronted him. There at the table sat Silu and Mindy doing homework together. Both smiled sheepishly as he entered having heard Jerry's voice out in the hallway.

"Hi Jerry. This is a surprise," Mindy said with an unconvincing smile.

"Obviously," Jerry replied flatly.

"We're trying to catch up on work missed while we've been away," Silu explained trying to pre-empt Jerry's interrogations. "Because we've both been away for a few days the teachers have sent work home to us."

"Looks very cosy," Jerry replied, wishing he hadn't come now. "I just came round to see how you were. I was worried about something Wayno said but I can see now I shouldn't have been."

"It's good to see you, Jerry," Mindy suddenly piped up. He looked at her sadly and decided not to speak in case his voice trembled and made him sound stupid.

"I've got to go now – I'm pretty busy." Jerry turned back towards the hallway.

"Why don't you stay and chat?" Mindy said with some urgency.

"Don't think so somehow." Jerry strode to the front door, opened it and stepped out closing it firmly behind him.

As he ambled away he heard the door open behind him, so he turned round to see Mindy and Silu standing on the stone step.

"We're both back tomorrow. Meet us by the front gates, please mate."

The last word and the pleading tone had an effect on Jerry who nodded before continuing his long walk home.

That evening he sat silently brooding and feeling less assured about the way things were going.

Chapter Seventeen

Before registration the next morning Jerry hung around by the front gate hoping to encounter Wayno. At first there was no sign of any of the usual crowd and Jerry found himself greeted by a great number of younger pupils who all seemed eager to be seen to know him.

To his dismay Rhino lumbered towards him with two mates slinking a few paces behind.

"Let me tell you something, four-eyes. I dunno what you said to Wayno but I ain't freakin-well scared of you."

"Tell your boss I want to talk to him. In the woods at the beginning of lunch." Jerry stared back with a smile.

"He ain't my boss," Rhino grumbled as he hawked some catarrh from his throat and gobbed it so it landed yellow and glistening a few inches from Jerry's feet.

"How delightful," Jerry said as he stepped over the wet blob and walked past Rhino and his henchmen.

After an uneventful morning Jerry headed straight off to the wooded area at the edge of the field as soon as they were dismissed from French.

Once at the perimeter scrubland Jerry slowed down and thought carefully about whether he should pass the first group of trees. He felt like a soldier about to enter enemy territory.

"Over here."

Jerry pushed his glasses on squarely to see who had spoken. Wayno stood before him heading a large gang of mobilised troops including Silu, Rhino and even Mindy. They all stepped out from behind the copse. So it seemed he'd been right not to trust Mindy; a fact which saddened him greatly.

Wayno seemed to be squinting slightly even though the sun remained behind a cloud cover.

"I don't know what sort of super-powers you think you have, but I'm ready for you this time, four-eyes."

Jerry looked on with disappointment.

"I'm not scared of you, Wayne Cadman. I've had you twice in a fight now. I thought maybe you'd had enough."

"There's more of us than you," Wayno sneered. "And I'll do your Paki mate next. I enjoyed giving your other friend a work out. He might be good at football but he's a crap fighter."

Jerry nodded. So Wayno did beat Matty up in some form of twisted vengeance.

Jerry put his hand in his pocket, felt the familiar shape of his mobile phone and recalled what he'd practised a number of times. Two presses of the top left hand button got him to contacts; then his finger found number 6, which is also the letter M. This got Matty's number on the screen then he found the larger 'Call' button. This prearranged system meant Matty would now go and get Mr Finn. Jerry had already warned Matty about the location of his potential danger.

"Too scared to fight me, eh? So you pick on my mates? You lot are cowards."

He just managed to complete the call before Rhino came roaring towards him. The rest of the gang hung back until reinforcements were required as the fight already looked uneven.

"This is it now, you freak. You and me, here. Let's finish this right now." Rhino held a fist up to Jerry's face. He could see the scars and bumps of knuckles frequently used for fighting. Jerry even had time to see some red lines on the lad's wrists and wonder if they came from previous punch-ups or as a result of self-harming.

At first Jerry assumed his new-found powers would protect

him so he stood calmly before the retracting fist. When he felt his nose explode and he realised his hands were scraping along the floor he understood he'd been punched directly.

He grunted and slumped to the floor. Something wet ran into his mouth and he put a dirty hand to his nose then looked at it to see lots of crimson blood. Wondering why Rhino didn't follow up with a second blow Jerry saw to his relief and delight that Silu had run up behind Rhino and thrown both arms bravely around his neck. This kept Rhino busy for a few moments as he flailed his arms wildly hoping to connect with Silu's head, but Silu proved to be deft and sprightly enough to avoid any serious blow. Jerry knew Rhino couldn't be held for long, but he took a quick look back out towards the field and the school. To his relief he saw Matty and Mr Finn jogging towards them. Rhino didn't see them but Wayno did.

Rhino and Silu were still grappling and struggling with Rhino obviously more powerful. To Jerry's disappointment Wayno and his mates kept their distance and just watched with fixed grins. Wayno seemed to squint and hold his head to one side blinking repeatedly.

Rhino screamed something to Wayno as he held Silu in a strangler's grip.

"Are you gonna help me out here? I'm doing this for you, ya bastard, and you just stand there watching."

To his surprise Wayno and his mates, rather than coming to help, began to shuffle furtively away, return to the field and walk back to school without looking back.

"Where the hell are you going you bloody cowards?" He looked up and saw Jerry, Matty and Mindy watching him. He didn't understand why his friends had scarpered and left him. "Help me kill this freakin' Paki. Best thing to do with 'em." He looked at Jerry then at Mindy as his grip tightened on Silu. "You and Wayno are both dirty Paki-lovers aren't you? It makes me sick. I wish we could exterminate the lot of 'em.

Drown 'em like rats." He looked down at Silu whose eyes began to bulge. "The best kind of Paki is a dead one."

"Let him go, Brian, or I will come over there and punch you into tomorrow. I have witnesses here who will back me up when I say it was in self-defence. Let the boy go."

Rhino looked confused. "Mr Finn? I didn't see you there." He let go of Silu and then looked up, perplexed by the sudden appearance of the giant Deputy Head. The teacher took another step towards him. Now he understood why the others had disappeared and left him.

"I've been standing here all the time, Brian – didn't you see me? And I heard all your despicable racist abuse. I think the governors will be very interested to hear your views on race relations. Did you know there are laws now about inciting racial hatred or violence? So this becomes a police matter too. You need to collect your belongings before you leave the premises because I can tell you now that you will never be coming back here."

Rhino seemed to be trying to compute the Deputy-Head's words and their complex meaning. First his eyebrows dipped in deep thought then his expression became one of anxiety, before returning to the aggressive pout familiar to Jerry and his many other victims.

"Come on then," he said to Mr Finn. "You can't touch me. If you do I'll sue you."

"Really? Is that right?" Finn replied with a chuckle in his throat. Without a moment's delay he ran towards Rhino, bent down and lifted him bodily onto his shoulder in a fireman's lift. Rhino screamed and kicked but couldn't move his arms.

Mr Finn turned round and began walking back to school.

"Could one of you lads run to the office and tell them to phone the police. Jerry would you be a good chap and grab this young hooligan's feet. Do you think you can manage that? Careful he doesn't kick you. Look I'll tell you what." Without a warning Mr Finn flicked Rhino off his shoulder and let him drop to the ground with a thump. With lightning speed he sat on Rhino's chest, looking down towards the boy's feet, ignoring the thumping he received on his back. Finn leaned down and held Rhino's legs with one hand. "Take his boots off will you, there's a good lad."

Jerry obediently unlaced Rhino's steel-capped Dr Martens, which Mindy picked up and carried without being asked. Once done Mr Finn threw Rhino back onto his shoulder and continued on his way. Jerry walked in front holding the boy's feet together, now made harmless in their dirty grey socks. And what a wondrous walk it was. Pretty much the entire school came over to see the spectacle and when they saw who had been captured and how ignoble he now seemed there came a roar of approval and a spontaneous burst of applause at the approaching champions: Jerry and Mr Finn.

Rhino was permanently excluded with immediate effect. In response to this famous victory Wayno made himself scarce and former victims began to believe that the fight against bullying had worked. Mr Finn sent Jerry and Silu to see the school nurse who checked them thoroughly. With the last game of the season coming Silu felt relieved to not be seriously injured.

"We mustn't get complacent," Jerry told the crowd who crushed in to the hall at the end of lunchtime. "We've won a battle but not the war," he announced, repeating the very phrase Quincy Finn had used in a conversation with him just ten minutes earlier. "It's true – Rhino has gone ... forever." Uproarious cheering ensued and Jerry held up a hand like a king silencing his subjects. "But he's not the only bully in this school." This comment met with nods and murmurs of approval. "The others might lie low for a while but they'll be back. So let's continue with the campaign and show all bullies everywhere that we are not weak – we will no longer allow ourselves to be victimised and made to feel worthless. We have feelings, talents and ideas of our own and we will be heard."

The applause and whoops soon got drowned out by percussive stamping and the chanting of "Bullies and bullying – OUT! OUT! OUT!"

Whilst hordes of children flowed out onto the pavement outside school creating currents, contra flows and slipstreams, Jerry hung onto the gatepost giving waves and smiles to those who acknowledged him.

"Good work today, Jerry."

"It's been much quieter this afternoon thanks to you."

"I saw you and Finn carry that bully. That was well cool."

"Is he really really gone?"

Jerry nodded, trying to look demure and modest. A moment later he became aware of mutterings as youngsters disappeared rapidly like ants retreating to a nest. Then he saw why. Wayno walked slowly towards him; not with his usual strut but with a more belligerent gait. When he reached his adversary he stopped and gave a pained and haunted look. Jerry watched as he squinted again slightly as if adjusting focus. The silence remained like a barrier between them, although the fact Wayno said nothing showed how things had already begun to change.

Jerry hung around for longer, sliding down the gate-post until he slumped on to the floor.

"Jerry? Jerry!"

"Sir Jerry," he murmured. "The Knight of Myopia."

"Jerry? You okay?"

"I am the champion riding on my black unicorn..."

"I think you're delirious, son. It's been a long day."

Jerry suddenly came to and realised Mr Finn spoke to him as he rocked Jerry's shoulder. Jerry shook his head – he'd been asleep. How embarrassing. "I'm okay, thanks," he said as he stood up straight, wobbling like a baby giraffe.

"Thank the Lord," Mr Finn exclaimed. "I saw you on the ground here from my office and thought you'd been stabbed or something."

Jerry laughed and felt grateful. "I'm fine thanks. I just fell asleep. Like you say sir, it's been a long and exhausting day."

"What are you doing here? Why don't you go home?"

"I was waiting for my friends," Jerry replied. His nose still felt sore but he'd been glad when the nurse had checked it and announced it to be merely bruised.

"Which friends, Jerry? You have so many." Mr Finn grinned down at him and extended an arm out to help Jerry balance. "You need to go home and rest."

"Silu and Mindy."

"Ah well, I can help you there. Sachindra got sent home to rest before the big game and Parminder is in a detention with Miss Powys. Would you like me to give you a lift home?"

"No thanks. I'll get the bus and then it's only a short walk."

"Well, if you're sure," Mr Finn said uncertainly and he waited, looking Jerry up and down as if undertaking a final health and safety assessment on a new building.

"Honestly, sir. It's okay. I feel absolutely fine. I think the little catnap really helped."

"Well, I'll leave you to it then." Mr Finn watched him carefully for a few seconds then executed a military about-turn. "Good night, Jerry." With that Quincy Finn pounded away like a giant returning to his lair. Jerry swore he could feel the ground vibrate with each step.

He decided to leave the school entrance with its prying cameras and exposure to the front offices and he turned left towards the wooded area, which he felt he now knew well. Wary at first, as he didn't know who might be in there, he quickly negotiated his way through and found himself on the edge of the school field where the spectacle occurred earlier that day.

It was then an easy run from there to the mobile classroom where he could guarantee no security cameras. The mobile classroom was cut off from the rest of school, like a boat adrift.

You couldn't even hear the bell or fire alarm in there. Using the hand rail he hauled himself up onto the platform that led to the door. It opened creakily and he stepped up to Miss Powys's door and looked through the sliver of glass. There sat Mindy and his form tutor just as expected. Jerry couldn't decide whether to knock or burst in, but decided on the former as being more appropriate. Once Miss Powys looked up he pushed the door open and stepped in. He relished the few moments of tension this created.

"Oh, hello Jerry. I assumed you'd gone home," Miss Powys said in surprise. "Have you forgotten something?"

"No miss," he answered, steadily trying to catch Mindy's gaze, but she refused to look up and continued doing her work. "I wanted to speak to Mindy." This caused Mindy to put down her pen and return his look.

"But she's doing a detention so you'll have to wait until she's finished," Miss Powys said abruptly.

"Okay," Jerry said, taken aback. "Can I wait here?"

"I suppose so. As long as you don't disturb our work. I've got lots of marking."

Jerry slumped down on a chair and took out his mobile phone.

When he looked back at Miss Powys he saw to his horror she had tears streaking her make-up as she slumped forwards with her forehead propped in her hand. Jerry and Mindy looked at each other with concern, shrugging and changing helpless expressions.

"Miss Powys?" Mindy got up first and stood next to her. She placed a palm on her shoulder. "Are you okay?"

Miss Powys blew her nose into a tissue and sat upright, staring ahead.

"Are you alright, miss?" Mindy spun round to Jerry who came up to the teacher's desk, shrugging.

Miss Powys blurted out suddenly. "I think something's wrong." She clutched her stomach.

"Is it the baby, miss?"

"Baby?" Mindy exclaimed. Jerry put a finger to his lips and Mindy stepped back.

Miss Powys wept fresh tears and began to sob, with tears forming pools on the wooden desk. "Oh god! Oh no! Please help me! Something's wrong with my baby."

"I'll get Mr Finn. He'll know what to do. You stay here." Jerry raced off whilst Mindy comforted the teacher now lost in convulsions of misery.

Mr Finn dealt with the whole situation calmly. He nodded seriously as Jerry explained the details and jogged ahead of Jerry to the classroom.

"I've called an ambulance. Oh Emma, my darling, why didn't you come to me straight away? Surely you know you could've spoken to me. I would have supported you right from the beginning." He knelt down and held her in a comforting embrace. "Trouble is the stupid ambulance could take ages. Tell you what, I'll drive you to the hospital myself. Wait here."

They marvelled to see Quincy Finn's car speed down the grassy slope towards them, churning up mud and chunks of turf. Mr Finn carried Miss Powys down the steps and got her into the passenger seat. Jerry put Miss Powys's bags into the boot.

"Take care, miss," Jerry called through the open hatchback before closing it.

"I can trust you two to go straight home now can't I?" Mr Finn asked. "Mindy, your detention has been served. I don't ever want to see you in another detention or I will personally speak to your father."

Mindy nodded. "Thank you, sir. I won't."

As the car drove off Jerry and Mindy were left alone together.

Chapter Eighteen

"Poor Miss Powys," Mindy said still staring at the spot where the car had last been seen before it turned the corner.

"Must've been awful - us wittering on all the time with all that going on in her private life." Jerry considered this for a few moments. "We don't really spend much time thinking about teachers as humans with their own lives at home."

"No," Mindy agreed, "I've never seen that side of Mr Finn before either."

"Isn't he great?" Jerry exclaimed proudly.

After a moment's silence, as both continued to stare at the last spot where Quincy Finn's car had been. Mindy broke the spell.

"Tell me how you knew Miss Powys was – you know – pregnant." Mindy's eyes narrowed suspiciously, forcing Jerry to snort with laughter.

"It's a long story and no it's definitely not what you're thinking! I'll tell you later once you've explained your love life to me."

"Oh yeah. That. I know how it looks but – no – I'm not going out with Wayno."

"But you kissed in front of me," Jerry said reliving the horror.

"Believe me it was hideous," Mindy shuddered. "I had to do it as part of the plan."

"What plan?" asked the incredibly relieved Jerry.

"Silu, Matty and I worked together. We couldn't tell you or it might not've worked."

Just as he felt himself about to yell out his complaint it occurred to Jerry how he hadn't exactly revealed everything he'd experienced recently to Mindy either.

"Why don't we phone Silu and see how he is? If he's back home we'll go and see him and we can tell you together."

"Hey, you know when I saw you two round his house? I thought..."

Mindy nodded. "I can see it would've looked suspicious but I'm really not that kind of girl. And anyway, Silu wouldn't hit on his best mate's girlfriend."

"So, is that what you are then? My girlfriend. I like the sound of that."

"You're my hero. I told you that before."

"Well, I don't feel like one. I was scared that you'd think me a real wimp who can't stand up for himself. I got embarrassed. Why would someone as gorgeous and lovely and intelligent as you be interested in a stupid geek like me?"

She took his hand in hers.

"Because you're not a stupid geek, Jerry Hough, and I won't have you saying it. Don't you get it? I think you're great precisely because you don't hit back. We should never hurt other people; never get revenge by fighting. It takes great courage to just get up and keep walking. Then when I saw you that day on the floor I didn't see a wimpy victim – I saw a real man who got up and brushed himself down. Just like my Dad. And as I've got to know you I've continued to like what I see."

He stepped right up to Mindy, placed one hand on her soft, warm cheek, brushed back her silky black hair with the other hand and then kissed her gently on the lips. She responded by wrapping both arms behind his back and pulling him closer until their bodies pressed tightly together. Jerry didn't ever want to move: he'd found his Utopia and it was a damn sight more real and enjoyable than Myopia.

"I promise not to doubt you again," he whispered close to her ear. Pleasingly this received another kiss then an intimate embrace, sharing each other's warmth for a few precious moments.

"So what's with this big plan then? You said you and Silu were going to explain it to me – at last."

"Let's go to his place and we can tell you."

"Shall we catch the bus?" Jerry offered with a smirk. "It's about as romantic as I can afford right now."

"Okay," Mindy replied with a tut. "Last one there's a ... goggly four-eyes!" She pulled Jerry back causing him to stumble and sprinted past him.

Silu opened the door, having got the text message Jerry sent from the bus.

"Thank God you're here. Let's go upstairs," he said pointing unnecessarily to the stairs. Then he lowered his tone to a stage whisper. "Mum and dad are in there getting all loved up on the sofa watching chick-flicks. Not a nice sight."

"Aah, that's well sweet," Mindy said with a distant look. Silu and Jerry swapped scowls.

"No it isn't." Silu led the way and they all ended up sitting on his bed which sported a Crawley FC duvet.

"When's the final?" Jerry asked. In all the recent excitement he'd forgotten about it.

"Next week," Silu said. "You and your dad gonna come round, right? My dad and Uncle Kamal will be here."

"That'd be great."

"Mindy? You gonna watch the big game?" Silu asked.

"I wouldn't want to miss a party, now." Mindy put her arm round Jerry's shoulder and he responded by curling his arm around her waist and placing his hand on her thigh. "Anyway we're here to apologise to Jerry. We have a lot of explaining to do."

"Yup, you're right there." Silu got up and paced the room like a lawyer. "You must've been wondering what the hell was going on." He ignored Jerry's purposeful nodding and continued his seemingly prepared speech. "We both agreed that you shouldn't know what we were doing. It wasn't because we don't trust you; just that Wayno had to believe in us. We thought we could get more information and ammo from him if he really believed we had turned away from you."

"Looking back now we were stupid and the idea of going out with him was a bit dangerous – I can see that now," Mindy blurted desperate for Jerry to understand.

"Mindy actually managed to stop him really hurting you," Silu explained. "If it wasn't for her, Wayno, Rhino and a whole gang of them were going to follow you after school one day and beat the crap out you. Mindy talked him out of it, but it took some doing."

"I hate to admit it but I had to let him kiss me with tongues and I just about stopped the little perv from groping me. Yuk."

Silu continued with his statement: "I had to convince him I didn't like you anymore and had to complete some stupid forfeits to get accepted. Poor Matty went through the same process but he was less willing and I think Wayno saw through his pretence. Bloody hell, he got a proper hiding I can tell you."

"So what exactly did you learn from this little plan of yours?"

Mindy and Silu exchanged glances.

"I feel a bit sorry for him actually," Mindy admitted.

"Sorry?" Jerry pulled a silly face. "After all he's done?"

"Girls, eh?" Silu said tapping a finger on the side of his head.

"What I mean is I think he's a bit unhappy."

"Good," Silu said abruptly. "He deserves to be."

"I think there's more to him than there seems. He always looks lonely and sad."

"He's a sad git, that's for sure," Silu with a laugh.

"No – maybe Mindy's got a point," Jerry said.

"You gone soft in the head too?" Silu asked.

"Okay, so Mindy stopped me getting my arse kicked in," Jerry said, trying to sort out the mass of thoughts cascading inside his head. "So why did you and Matty have to turn into complete plonkers then?"

"Because Rhino threatened us and our families. He was gonna hurt Prabs – you know, my little cousin. We had to prove we didn't like you any more – which is hard when you go saving me in the playground," Silu said giving Jerry a high-five. "You're the best mate a bloke could have."

"Oh stop it, darling," Jerry replied in a mock camp voice. "I'm filling up here."

"Although if you ever talk to me with that voice again I'll have to beat the crap out you myself," Silu replied with a big grin.

"Nuff said," Jerry answered, holding up his hand and feigning fear. "What I still don't understand is why you didn't tell me. I can keep a secret or pretend and act ignorant."

"You don't need to pretend or act, mate," Silu chipped in quickly, making Mindy guffaw.

"Yeah yeah, whatever. So what did you actually learn then in this death-defying undercover job then?" Jerry put his chin in his hand and gave a wide-eyed, expectant look.

"Ah," Silu replied in a deep voice, scratching his neck ponderously. "Very little really. I got his address and mobile number."

"Did you go to his house?" Jerry asked.

"Er, no. I wasn't exactly invited in for a cuppa." Silu laughed at the thought. "I don't think Wayno is the kind of guy to invite you round for tea and cakes."

Jerry chewed his bottom lip deep in thought.

"What are you thinking about?" Mindy asked him having seen his expression.

"That's what I need to do, to understand what's going on in his head."

"What are you blabbing on about?" Silu asked.

"I remember something Stephen said to me," Jerry began. "The best way to resolve a problem is to sit down with your enemy and have a drink or a meal together. Eating together gives you a chance to talk things through. And if we meet him in his own territory then he won't feel threatened and he may open up. It's worth a try."

"If you go round he'll just beat you up."

"No he won't," Jerry said confidently.

"Then I'll come with you," Silu insisted.

"And he listens to me," Mindy said.

"But what if he realises he's lost you back to Jerry? Wayno'll go ballistic."

"He's got a point," Jerry said nodding. "We'll break that news to him some other time."

"So when do we go?"

Jerry looked at his watch as if making some important calculation. "No time like the present."

"Have you actually thought this through?" Mindy asked nervously putting a hand out towards him. "What are you going to say exactly?"

"Don't worry," Jerry said as Mindy got up to kiss him on the lips. "I'll be as nice as pie."

Silu stood up and looked at Mindy. "What about me? Do I get a kiss?"

Jerry stepped between them facing his friend.

"Oh go on then. Thought you'd never ask."

It took ten minutes to walk there briskly. Silu pointed out a small block of two storey flats standing in the middle of an otherwise terraced road lined with rowans.

"The downstairs left flat," Silu said.

"Are you sure?" Jerry asked scanning the building like an expert cat-burglar. All the curtains were closed.

"I came here with him and a few others when he went to get some money off his old man. He made us all wait out here but we could still hear the shouting."

Jerry thought for a few moments before speaking.

"So what will Wayno do when he sees you with me? Don't want to make trouble for you unnecessarily."

"Yeah but I've been such a rubbish friend to you recently," Silu said with some regret. "I need to make up for it. I don't care if he doesn't like it. You're my real mate, Jerry and I'm gonna stick with you whatever. So don't argue."

This made Jerry grin inanely.

He led the way down a short path between an unkempt lawn of clover and dandelions, under an arched doorway, past some steep stone stairs to the first floor flats and then turned left to find the last door. It had no bell or number, just flaking faded blue paintwork and a rusty letter box.

"Sure anyone lives here?" Jerry said, pulling a face. Silu nodded, clearly trying not to look nervous.

"Righty then," Jerry flexed his fingers before making them into a fist with the index knuckle protruding. He rapped loudly on the middle wooden panel of the door. The first sound was a deep growl then a loud bark from inside the flat, followed by the skittering of claws on a hard floor as a dog ran towards the noise. More barking ensued as the dog pounded onwards, before hurling itself at the wooden door with an enormous echoing bang and a yelp. It made the two boys step back nervously. A whining sound came from behind the door now as the dog obviously licked its wounds. Then it resumed its barking non-stop.

"Well that should alert any occupants," Jerry said with a slow nod.

"An effective burglar alarm," Silu agreed.

Over the barking came a man's voice.

"Shut up you stupid mutt!"

The dog ignored the voice and carried on; this time also bashing its paws rapidly against the door as if trying to tunnel out to reach its new found prey outside.

More yelping could be heard and Jerry could only assume the man was hitting it.

"Get back dammit!"

After more yelps and a long whine, it sounded like the dog was being dragged away and restrained somehow. Then bolts were pulled behind the door they still stood facing and both boys felt a change of mood, becoming less certain about their poorly thought through mission.

The faded blue door shuddered into life and they found themselves confronted by a huge bald man in a string vest and boxers staring through small puffy eyes.

"What the bloody hell do you want?"

Jerry lost any vestige of confidence and it took all his will not to stutter.

"Um, is Wayne there?"

"What's it got to do with you?"

"We'd like to speak to him."

The man looked quickly at Jerry and then turned his attention to Silu. He peered menacingly at him from head to toe and then looked back at Jerry.

"My Wayne ain't friends with no wog."

"Excuse me?" Jerry responded in disbelief.

"How do I know he ain't some sort of Ayrab terrorist?"

Silu stood his ground. "I'm not an Arab – not even a Muslim."

The man looked non-plussed. "Yeah but you're from Pakiland ain't ya?"

"No," Silu countered. "I was born in Guildford, Surrey."

Jerry put a hand on his friend's shoulder. "Leave it buddy. It's not worth the aggro."

"If you're his buddy," the man said to Jerry, "then you can bugger off too."

Silu stepped backwards a few yards. "It's okay," he nodded to Jerry. "I don't want trouble. You carry on. I'll stay over here."

"That's it Ghandi," the repulsive man shouted. "Get back to

152

Fuzzy-wuzzy world with all your suicide bomber mates."

Silu pressed his fingers into his eyes as if weeping for the state of the world.

"Is Wayno in?" Jerry asked, standing in front of Silu so as to distract the man he assumed to be Wayno's dad.

"Yeah, but he's busy right now. So you two girls sod off and don't come back here," he made a point of peering over Jerry's shoulder at Silu. "My son ain't no paki-lover"

Jerry turned away feeling he didn't even want to waste any more time here. As they wandered back to Silu's house in silence he began thinking about Wayno again and wondering...

Once logged onto Facebook, Jerry clicked on the link where it said 'Chat'. Three of his friends were online including the one he was hoping for: Mindy Sidhu. He clicked the left mouse button on her name and it gave him a box for an instant message.

'really sorry about all the recent crap dunno what came over me'
Her reply only took a few seconds.

'no im sorry i been a bit of a div'

'maybe we both been a bit pants'. Jerry hoped this wouldn't offend her and regretted sending it when she didn't respond immediately. A few minutes passed until he heard a pop like a bubble bursting.

'lol – we been really rubbish but now hope things r sorted????'
Jerry grinned

'everythings just dandy ;-)'

'everyone makes mistakes' said Mindy's next message in the dialogue box. *'suppose we should learn from mistakes & not make the same ones again'.*

Jerry read the words a few times.

'u sound like my mum lol' Jerry typed with a real laugh.

'dont 4get 2 brush ur teeth & wash behind ur ears then!!'

This comment created a natural lull. Jerry was in the middle of typing a question to continue the discussion when Mindy beat him to it.

'whats ur next move gonna b?'

Jerry deleted the message he'd started which seemed no longer appropriate and typed an answer to her question which he hoped didn't give too much away.

'if u wanna sort out a problem seek out the source says my Dad - when we had wasps it was no good just killing individual insects we had to get rid of the nest'

'what u on about? u on drugs? Not gonna kill Wayno r u?'

'just need 2 get into the nest 2 find some answers'.

'think u need a good night sleep – you lost the plot my darling'.

Jerry got excited when he saw the last two words.

'c ya gorgeous'.

'ciao for now handsome – sweet dreams'.

Jerry felt sure his dreams would be particularly sweet; especially with her as their leading lady.

Friday morning seemed odd without Miss Powys, but to Jerry's delight his tutor group's register was taken by Mr Finn. They all sat silently in neat rows as the Deputy Head led them in a short informal 'assembly' which involved a few words about team-work and how they all had to pull together and help each other in Miss Powys's absence.

"The good news is that her baby is absolutely fine."

There followed a big cheer from the entire group.

Mr Finn finished tutor time with a prayer asking God to give her inner strength. The chant of 'Amen' at the end was loud and enthusiastic. Vicki volunteered to buy a card over the weekend for them all to sign and Mr Finn promised to take it to her on Monday evening.

After an uneventful day of predictable lessons Jerry went to his locker to retrieve the books he would need for homework over the weekend and waited a few minutes for the masses to subside until there were only a few people left. He waved when he saw Silu and Matty appear.

"Hi," Jerry said. "Something important's come up. I need you to cover for me."

"What you up to?" Silu asked frowning.

"I told my mum I was going to the cinema with you after school," Jerry explained putting his hand on Silu's arm. "Just in case she phones your mum could you be out and tell them you're at the cinema with me. Go to Matty's house or something. Is that okay ... with both of you?"

"Yeah, course," Silu agreed and Matty nodded cheerfully.

"What are you going to do?" Silu asked.

"I'll tell you later," Jerry replied, "I just need you to trust me on this one."

"You're going to his place aren't you?"

Jerry raised his eyebrows mysteriously, swung his bag over his shoulder and wandered off into the unknown.

"Be careful, mate," came Silu's voice.

Chapter Nineteen

Jerry stood outside Wayno's door for a while before summoning up the courage to rap confidently on the blue, flaky door. All he knew was that he must somehow get into Wayno's flat. For what felt the first time in his life Jerry allowed his instinct to dictate his actions. It just seemed the right thing to do.

If Wayno's dad answered the door then he'd hold his nerve and walk away then wait for a good opportunity. Jerry had seen Wayno walk a different way off towards the park so he knew he was not home.

The first noise he heard was the dog scrabbling towards the door and then leaping up and down yapping loudly, which made Jerry's heart leap and then sink. Perhaps he wasn't ready for this. He patted his pocket to check his supplies and steeled himself for his next move.

Jerry's head began to ache with the cold.

The next phase involved getting inside.

In his mind's eye Jerry saw himself as the Knight of Myopia stealthily slipping through a window and into the lair of the beast, ready to face his greatest fear in the final confrontation. With the image lodged in his mind he moved across to the flat's windows on the right of the door. They were frosted and patterned suggesting it was the bathroom. On tiptoes Jerry reached up to the small top window and slipped a finger in a slim gap at the bottom frame. Pinching the window he managed to wiggle it slightly which loosened it, much to his surprise. With a better grip on it he found that with another few shakes it worked loose completely, opening fully with its metal window stay swinging unhooked.

Jerry wondered if this was a coincidence or if he had somehow 'willed' it to happen.

Checking nobody could see him, but feeling confidently hidden from the public gaze, he used the small window sill to sit on whilst he hauled himself up head first through the small rectangular hole. Managing to squeeze his shoulders through easily, it became quickly apparent that he might not get the rest of himself in quite so easily. However with one arm through he could easily reach down and unhook the arm of the stay on the larger window and lift the fastener to allow the large window to swing open towards him. Then it became a simple matter of climbing in as quickly and safely as possible. He felt grateful there were not lots of things on the window-sill to knock over or tread on.

When he heard the dog, however, he began to lose his nerve. He stood his ground without letting the yapping or skittering of paws concern him. The dog skidded on the hall's parquet flooring and came rushing into the bathroom where Jerry stood frozen. It looked like some scruffy cross-breed bull terrier. It stopped when it saw Jerry and began to growl deeply, but Jerry had come prepared with some cold ham and more than a little optimism.

Slowly and with no sudden movements he pulled a clear plastic food bag out of his pocket and dipped one hand inside. Jerry tore off a chunk of ham and held it out towards the still growling mutt. After pointing its snout in the air the dog crept gingerly towards Jerry putting faith in his olfactory senses. With the chunk of ham dangling from the tips of his fingers, Jerry watched the bull terrier creep gradually closer until its nose touched the meat. Without warning the dog barked loudly, making Jerry jerk the ham backwards. The dog gave a little jump following the meat's trajectory and, instinctively, Jerry flipped the ham in the air in preference to losing some fingers.

To his immense relief the dog took most interest in the ham and attacked it rather than Jerry. Still growling, but now possibly with pleasure, the mutt skittered round in circles chasing the elusive meat, finally catching it and swallowing it with a quick nod and couple of snaps. Then to Jerry's amusement the dog turned back to him and sat back on his hind legs, with fore-paws up as if to beg for more. Luckily Jerry had brought a whole pack of processed ham, hoping his mum wouldn't notice its mysterious disappearance. The next chunk was gratefully received by the now happy dog who tucked in with his tail wagging. As he ate Jerry bravely leaned down and patted the creature, careful to only touch him on the top of his head well away from its salivating jaws. When the dog responded to his touch Jerry knew that he had won the first round and the next bit of ham was offered on his open palm. The dog took it carefully, swallowed it and then licked Jerry's hand, before sitting up nicely again, this time with tongue hanging out and his tail wagging happily.

Jerry patted him again and tickled his ear before spreading out the rest of the ham on the linoleum floor. It seemed funny that such a vicious dog should respond so readily to something as simple as food and a bit of kind attention; however the plan, which could have gone horribly wrong, worked. Jerry's instinct had been right. It was as if he'd had some kind of inner knowledge.

Jerry could not help but like the dog, now so friendly and full of character. Once the ham had disappeared the dog then turned to its new friend in the hope of playing or at least for further attention. This time Jerry stroked him further down his neck and onto his back. He felt some rough bumps and as his hand brushed over them the dog gave a little twitch . Jerry gently pushed up some of his white, flecked hairs and saw that the dog had red lines and scars across his back. When it rolled over wanting to be tickled more Jerry saw more sores and abrasions.

"Good boy, you are. You poor old thing you. You look like you've been hurt, old boy. You need a hug don't you, mate?"

Jerry drew closer and the dog jumped up onto all four and responded to the approaching Jerry by licking his face. The lad had to remove his glasses and give them a clean, giggling to himself as he tickled the dog's chin.

With the dog's confidence won, he decided to have a quick look round the flat to get his bearings. The danger was far from over and he would have to keep a keen ear open for anybody returning home. With the dog faithfully at his heels he had a quick look in each room, still uncertain exactly what he was looking for.

In the main lounge he saw a large cage in the corner, presumably for the dog. It was made of thick wire mesh, spacious enough for the dog to move and leap around in. Otherwise the flat held no obvious secrets or surprises. It certainly looked untidy and grimy though, Jerry decided.

Just as he considered which bedroom he could hide in, the dog began barking and bouncing energetically. It then ran towards the door and Jerry realised somebody had put a key in the lock and was about to enter. Jerry darted into the nearest bedroom and with a baseball type slide secreted himself under the bed. He had no time to be concerned by the dirt, cobwebs, junk and smell surrounding him.

The door slammed shut and the dog barked, then yelped and whimpered. To Jerry's dismay the dog then scuttled into the room where he hid and lay down by the bed a few feet away from him.

"Shut up you stupid bloody mutt," yelled a man's voice. Into the bedroom appeared the same man Jerry had spoken to the day before. Jerry could see the bottom of his ripped jeans and his steel toe-capped boots. Jerry watched as he sauntered about the room looking even more confrontational with a fixed grimace screwing up his eyes and mouth. Wayno's dad proceeded to peel off his top to expose his hairy and protruding belly. Jerry knew his best bet lay with staying perfectly still. What frightened him the most was that the stupid dog might give him away. For the first time Jerry wondered what the hell he was doing in there.

Wayno's dad flicked his head round like a lizard, assessed the situation quickly and responded by kicking the dog squarely in the midriff. This caused the poor beast to roll a few times and then lunge into the corner where it whined pitifully and licked its sore patch. The man didn't seem to be finished with it though and Jerry wanted to call out. Instead he watched the brute of a man pounce upon it and grab it round the neck with one hand and collect all four paws in the other. The dog fought bravely with a manic struggle but was clearly no match for the human at least four times its size. It seemed to be overpowered when it suddenly twisted its head round and bit Wayno's dad on the arm.

With a shriek and a cascade of expletives the man flung the dog against the wall where it collapsed in a heap, struggled swiftly to its feet and limped out of the room to some hidey-hole.

"Stupid dickhead mutt," Wayno's dad snarled as he checked himself in a mirror hanging on the wall. He pressed his fingers against his arm and investigated the blood that came away, which to Jerry's disgust he licked. Once done, he posed at his reflection like a body-builder, pushing his elbows out and his fists together. Then with some effort he pulled in his excessive belly. After a smile and a nod of appreciation he left the room, closing the bedroom door behind him.

Jerry needed time for recuperation. Once he'd steadied his nerves he inched slowly forward on his belly like a worm, only stopping when he heard the dog bark again. After an indiscernible shout from his master, silence resumed. He gradually made his way out from the bed, as silently as possible, towards the door which he opened painfully slowly until it seemed wide enough for him to look through. His movement now, he decided, might well be limited by the presence of the dog. Once he'd pushed the door open a little way – enough to see out of – he scuttled back under the bed like a nervous insect. But now he could just see through the open door straight into the living room from where the television suddenly blasted into life.

Wayno's dad sat in an armchair drinking lager from a can whilst watching some game show and then Jerry could just make out part of the large wire cage containing the crestfallen dog presumably locked in. After a while Jerry closed his eyes and wondered if would ever get out alive. This must be the most stupid plan ever devised by any living being, he thought, as all hope began to slowly dissipate.

Jerry felt palpable relief when he heard a key scraping in the lock and heard the door swing open with a crash. Wayno stepped into the hallway only a few feet away from where Jerry hid.

"Bubbles? Where's my boofle Bubbles then?" Wayno said in a silly voice Jerry had never heard before. "Oi, dad! Where's Bubbles?"

Jerry had to hold his nose to stop himself sniggering aloud. So Wayno was capable of feelings after all then – if not for human beings.

Jerry watched the bully pad into the sitting room, wary in case Bubbles was let out of his cage.

Wayno's dad slid his eyes in his son's general direction.

"Where you been you little dick-head?"

"Nowhere."

"Bollocks - lying bastard."

"Been with Rhino," Wayno sniffed.

"His dad says the pigs been sniffin' round their gaff," his dad growled. "You do anything to bring rozzers round here and I'll rip your head off, you hear me?"

"I'm not stupid," Wayno replied.

"Yeah, right." His dad sniggered and turned the volume right up on the television. "Oi, get me another beer, you sad little fairy," he shouted, throwing the empty can at Wayno.

The boy obediently trotted into the kitchen and returned with another can the same colour, which the dad devoured in one swig before burping deeply with gusto. Wayno sidled up to the cage containing Bubbles and put his finger through the wire to tickle the dog's ear. Bubbles perked up suddenly and began panting and wagging his tail.

"Can I let him out now?"

"No," his dad exclaimed with unnecessary force. "The little bastard bit me." He held out his still bleeding arm. "He can die and rot in hell for all I care. He should be bloody put down." Wayno's dad laughed, crushed the empty can and threw it at his son. "I'll kill him myself next time you go out."

Without being asked Wayno went and got another beer and handed it silently over.

"Please don't hurt Bubbles, dad." Wayno sat on the sofa eating a packet of crisps he'd found in the kitchen cupboard.

"You sound like a right nonce," the man said. Then he put on a high-pitched mocking voice. "Oh puhlease don't hurt my fluffy little doggy. Anyway his name isn't Bubbles, it's Demon. He was a fighting dog once."

"Yeah, but he's in retirement now and he's a good guard dog – you gotta admit," Wayno said looking happy for the first time.

"He's a pain in the arse – just like you – and one day I'll kill him with my bare hands ... especially if he ever craps in the bedroom again."

"That was because you locked him in there. You're always horrible to him. That's why he bit you."

Wayno's dad got up with a look of fury.

"What the hell did you say?" He advanced towards Wayno. "Who the hell do you think you're talking to? Are you arguing with me, you dickhead?"

Wayno began to back off until he reached the dog's cage.

"No – I'm not arguing. Honest."

Wayno's dad downed a gulp of beer and returned to his chair.

"Can I let him out, dad? Please?" Wayno pleaded. "I'll take him out for a walk. It'll do him good."

His dad stared at the dog in the cage as the television continued blaring.

"Yeah, alright," his dad sniffed waving a hand like some emperor graciously granting a criminal his freedom.

Wayno jumped up and flicked a catch on the outside of the cage. Bubbles cowered further back against the wire mesh – uncertain what would happen next. Jerry squinted and had to move his head around to watch closely as Wayno coaxed the dog with a gentle voice and by rubbing his thumb and forefinger together. The soft words turned into a kissing noise then a clicking. He smiled when the dog slowly snuffled forward to lick his hand.

"Come on boy. Everything's okay. Do you want walkies?" Wayno spoke in a high-pitched voice, which startled Jerry. Bubbles jumped up and began panting excitedly. "Walkies yeah? Does that sound good? Does it boy? Come on then, let's get your lead, there's a good boy."

Wayno moved towards the hallway with Bubbles jogging close to his feet. On the way out Wayno had to pass his dad's chair and he made the mistake of not putting himself between his dad and the dog.

The man lifted his feet up to let the dog run underneath, but then suddenly crashed his heavily booted heels right into Bubble's back, practically folding the oblivious animal in two with a machine-gun crack of the bones. For Wayno the whole move was so unexpected he jumped in a mixture of confusion and horror. Jerry too had to cover his mouth to avoid giving himself away. Bubbles remained on the floor inert and silent.

Wayno saw the lifeless pile of fur then looked frantically left and right as if trying to understand the last few minutes. His look of hatred towards his dad shocked Jerry.

"You bastard! I hate you so much!"

"What did you call me?" The man stood up to his full height and stepped right up to Wayno, his eyes seething with anger. "Say that again, come on!"

At this point he began sparring with his son, except the jabs really connected. Wayno tried to defend himself with little effect and soon his nostrils ran with trickles of blood and the fleshy parts around the eyes quickly puffed up. When he collapsed onto the floor with hands uselessly held out over his face the man continued to punch him mercilessly and Jerry could take no more. He rolled out from under the bed, shoved open the door then ran into the room and leapt onto the man's back pulling his huge muscular arms back with all his might. Wayno's dad halted temporarily in his vicious assault and swatted back at Jerry as if dealing with an annoying fly.

Wayno was curled up into a ball, eyes closed as if ready to give up on this life. Jerry pummelled the man who turned confused, but managed to grab Jerry's wrists. The pain became unbearable until suddenly he saw the man's head fly backwards as if yanked by some unseen force. Wayno's dad let go of Jerry and fell to the ground.

Then Jerry realised that Wayno had sprung up and saved him. Wayno sat on top of his dad punching him harder and harder on his face and chest. Wayno's arms lashed again and again in an uncontrollable fury and Jerry could see the that the man underneath no longer responded.

"Wayno! Stop! Stop." He stepped up behind Wayno and put his hands on the other boy's shoulders. As calmly as possible he whispered in the raving boy's ear:

"Stop now, Wayne. It's all over. You can stop. Ssshhhh. Calm down mate."

Wayno responded to the calm voice and lowered his arms, shaking and breathily heavily. Jerry stepped away, allowing him a few moments to get his bearings and come back to reality. Wayno looked down at his dad who lay sobbing and bleeding beneath him and got up and moved over to his dad's chair where he collapsed.

"Are you okay?" He could see the boy's eyes were already puffed and heavily bruised.

"Where the hell did you come from?" Wayno stared unblinkingly with a grateful look in his bruised and darkened eyes.

Jerry stayed quiet and saw the boy he had previously hated with completely new eyes.

"What about your dad?"

Wayno gave a quick glance. "He's still alive worse luck."

"It's all over now." It was all Jerry could think of to say.

Wayno shook his head. "He never gives up on a fight. When he comes round he'll kill us. I mean he will murder us."

"So what should we do? You could come back to my place." Jerry felt it was the least he could do.

"No. This ends here. Now. Help me put him in the cage and then we'll call the police."

The two boys worked together hauling the semi-conscious man – a hefty weight – into the dog cage. With a final shove they got the door closed and Wayno locked it with some relish.

"Let me outta here, you bloody freak!" the man screamed, banging violently on the sides. Jerry worried what might happen if he got out, but the cage remained steadfast.

"Is he okay in there?" Jerry asked uncertainly as the man began screaming expletives again and whacking his head against the wire mesh with a rattling crash.

"He's put me in there enough times," growled Wayno angrily.

Jerry recalled having his mobile phone in his pocket and he rang 999. Once done he looked down at the weeping figure of Wayno now sprawled on the floor beside the bleeding dog's corpse. Wayno slowly looked up, getting to his hands and feet, whilst his dad shrieked continuously, slamming the cage into the wall in fury.

"You go, Jerry. You don't need to be involved in this at all. They'll believe me over him any day. Go. No point in you getting into any trouble." Wayno jerked hid head in the direction of the door. "You saved me man. I'll never forget it. Thanks. Now get outta here."

Once he heard the sirens, Jerry ran off outside into a darkly shimmering mist.

Chapter Twenty

Now Jerry felt incredibly guilty. What would happen to Wayno? If the police and social services got involved then he'd probably be taken to a home. Now all Wayno's bitterness and desire to hurt others made some kind of sense. But had he improved things or made them worse?

As soon as Jerry arrived at the school gates on Monday morning, complete with its Spex2Skool Day banner, he fell about laughing. He'd never seen such an amazing array of eyewear and optical instruments. There were glasses, shades, spectacles, half-rims, bifocals, pince-nez, monocles, visors, 3D glasses, horn-rims, browlines, cateyes, swimming and diving goggles, lorgnettes, raybans and even a welding mask. One boy had attached binoculars to his head which caused him to stumble blindly and hilariously about. The frames came in every shape, size and colour imaginable. The lenses were dark, light, shaded, mirrored or often non-existent. Some people dressed as famous glasses-wearers: including more than one Groucho Marx with comedy moustache, plastic nose and cigar attached to silly specs; some girls and one brave boy came as Dame Edna Everage with ornate, bejewelled fancy frames. Others became apparent too – namely Harry Potters, John Lennons and Rolf Harrises, whilst a few cheated slightly by wearing a pirate's eye-patch. Silu came in with gigantic plastic frames the size of two dinner plates and Matty had bought a joke pair of black round glasses with ridiculously thick lenses which magnified his pupils massively creating an absurd and hilarious effect.

At registration the tutor group milled about noisily laughing at everyone's appearance whilst waiting for Quincy Finn. When they saw him ascending the ramp they all calmed down and stood behind their chairs so that when he opened the door he was met by a quiet class. Jerry felt disappointed to see he hadn't made an effort to get into the spirit of Spex2Skool Day. Mr Finn looked around sternly.

"You may sit down."

With the grating sound of chairs scraping, the class sat down and Jerry saw Mr Finn sit down too and bend down beneath his own desk. Then Mr Finn stood up suddenly and the class burst into laughter. He had put on a black pair of spectacles with false, googly bug-eyes. When he nodded his head the googly eyes fell down and flew back up again on springs. He made them bounce up and down to much hilarity and even kept them on to call the register.

"Good morning year 10," he said in a slightly silly voice. "Today - and for today only! - you can call me Quincy."

The group answered the register with responses such as "Yo, Quincy, dude" or other similar exclamations, all said in a spirit of fun.

"Well you all look great today," Mr Finn said in his normal voice keeping on his comedy specs which had one eye up and one hanging down. "Let's not get carried away today, but try to remember that there is a point to all this. We are doing this in our continuing campaign to put a stop to bullying and we have the very man who started it all here in our very midst. Let's give him a round of ammunition ... sorry ... I mean a round of applause." Laughter interspersed with clapping as Jerry beamed at the acknowledgement, even receiving some pats on the back – although one came as more of a thump.

"Okay then kiddiwinks it's assembly time. I know it'll be worth staying awake for this morning because ... I'm taking it. Let's have shirts tucked in. Right, off you go then." He removed the glasses and put them in his briefcase.

On the way to the hall, they had to negotiate a few corridors and Jerry wondered who the adults were standing at various points en route.

"Know who this dodgy-looking lot are Jerry?" asked Mr Finn who had caught up with them. Jerry shook his head. "These are your body-guards. You know, the parents who volunteered to police the corridors and take shifts to help teachers stop conflicts and bullying." Jerry glowed with the thought of another of his ideas coming to fruition.

"Cool. And my dad's agreed to help on Friday lunchtimes. He gets off work early."

"Yes I was going to mention about your dad," Mr Finn continued as they walked together. "A position has come up for a Parent Governor and I think your dad is just the person for the job. Should I give him a call tonight and chat to him about it?"

"He's got lots of ideas for improving the school, that's for sure."

"Yes, I certainly got that impression, which is exactly why we need him. I'll give him a ring and we can go out for a beer."

"Oh, he'll like that," Jerry said with a knowing smile.

"Marvellous," the Deputy Head replied without breaking step.

Once at the hall, Mr Finn peeled off to stand on the stage at the front, whilst Jerry ran to catch up with his tutor group to file silently into the hall. Quincy Finn stood glaring seriously at a thousand children all wearing silly glasses. A few brave - or stupid – children dared mutter behind raised hands but the majority came in with a patient, respectful hush; mostly out of fear of being sent to the Deputy Head's office where they would be forced to wait in terrified anticipation.

"Good morning everyone."

"Good morning, Mr Finn," chanted a thousand voices in

unison.

"The Lord be with you."

"And also with you," chanted most of the teachers plus half-a-dozen keen pupils.

"You're looking really great this morning. I want to welcome you all to Spex2Skool Day. I'm sure everyone knows what it's all about. We're raising awareness about the horrors of bullying and today we're attempting something called empathy. A certain pupil in our midst – and Jerry Hough asked me not to mention his name, so I shan't … oops, sorry," Mr Finn raised a hand to his mouth pretending to have made a slip of the tongue. A titter rippled around the hall. "That certain pupil, whoever he is, raised the issue and told us he was being bullied because of his glasses, so today reminds us of a few things: firstly, how horrible bullying is. It is nasty, selfish, painful, thoughtless and brutish. Victims of bullying suffer both physically and psychologically and I want to explain right now in very clear terms that we will NOT accept any form of bullying in this school – be it violent, verbal or even cyber-bullying, which we will talk about another time. So let me state it very simply. This school has a zero-tolerance policy regarding bullying.

"Secondly, Spex2Skool Day reminds us that we don't choose to be born short-sighted, blind, deaf, handicapped or disabled as much as we have no choice as to whether we're born male, female, black, white, tall or short. When we meet a person with special needs or someone in a wheelchair we shouldn't laugh or judge them. Nor should we feel superior. Rather we should get on our knees and thank our creator that we are so lucky. If someone arrived now in this hall in a wheel-chair I wonder how you would react. Would you pity them? Mock them? Ignore them? Feel embarrassed? Patronise them?" Mr Finn paused for a long moment to allow the rhetorical questions to have their intended effect. "Who here has heard of Stephen Hawking?" A few hands shot up. "You've probably seen his cartoon representation on 'The Simpsons'. He is almost completely paralysed with a condition called neuro-muscular dystrophy and he can only speak through an electronic voice synthesiser, and yet he is one of the most brilliant scientists that ever lived – probably on a par with Einstein. He'd be offended if you went up to him and talked to him like a baby. Who here watches the Paralympics? It's a wonderful celebration of the fine achievements of athletes who have refused to feel sorry for themselves and gone on to achieve greatness like Tanni Grey-Thompson.

"Now I'm going to let you in on a secret. I was once a scrawny skinny kid with glasses and a squint." Jerry looked up in astonishment. Mr Finn seemed to be smiling right at him. "I was bullied because I was very tall and lanky, but I decided at an early age not to let it get me down or affect me. I remember sitting down one day wondering what a skinny tall lad could be successful at and my dad took me to see the Harlem Globetrotters playing basketball which clinched it for me. I bought a ball and a hoop and I practised and practised every single moment I had. My parents bought me contact lenses, which in those days were expensive and uncomfortable. We didn't do basketball at school but I joined a local team and worked hard at my game. Then my proudest moment came when I got selected to play for Great Britain. We weren't great and we lost most of our games but that didn't matter. Just having that shirt on my back made me feel very proud. But then injury put paid to my basketball career so I became a PE teacher. Some of you may think I felt disappointed – but no. Being Deputy Head here is really the best job in the world. Every working day I feel proud when I see you all trying your best and helping each other. I want you all to know how proud I am to see you grow, develop and mature into wonderful people. Not a day goes by when I don't thank God for giving me the best job in the world."

The hush in the hall was electric. Jerry had never heard such intense silence before. A few pupils sniffed and dabbed their moist eyes.

"I know what you're all wondering now," Mr Finn continued in a lighter tone. "Where are my glasses?" He turned his back to them all, reached down into his briefcase, stood up and turned to face them. Even though Jerry knew what was coming he still found it hilarious. Quincy Finn stood bobbing to and fro as the googly eyes bounced up and down on their ridiculously stretchy springs. The hall exploded into mirth, excitement and delight.

"Tutors, please let your groups out a line at a time from the back," Mr Finn bellowed from behind his comedy specs. "Have a good day everyone."

From the speakers piped the song *Proud* by Heather Small with its spine-tingling lyrics: 'What have you done today to make you feel proud?'

The big buzz of the day occurred when their local MP took a tour round the school with Mr Finn, followed by BBC cameras. Word spread round quickly that their school might be in the local news that night after the six o'clock news. Then came the local papers, the Crawley News and Observer, and even a DJ from Mercury FM who interviewed pupils in the playground and asked for requests and dedications. Jerry's proudest moment came when he was approached by the DJ who had been pointed in his direction.

"Hi, Jerry? Someone tells me you're the guy who started this whole Spex2Skool thing. Is that right?"

Jerry cleared his throat and leaned in to the proffered microphone.

"Well lots of others helped out – I didn't do it alone. Mr Finn and Miss Powys have to be thanked – good luck Miss P if you're listening. Then there are lots of others too, but I'd really like to thank one special person."

"Perhaps we could dedicate the next song to them?" the DJ

suggested.

"Yeah. This is for you, Mindy."

The DJ winked, smiled and lifted the mike back to his lips.

"That was Jerry Hough – local hero."

Chapter Twenty-One

At lunchtime, Jerry wandered around the school like a celebrity doing walkabout on the red carpet. Some year sevens even asked for his autograph. He decided to look for Wayno but he didn't have to try very hard as Wayno quickly found him.

"Jerry," he called in a distinctly unthreatening voice. When Jerry turned he felt delighted to see Wayno smile and wave at him. "Can we talk? Alone?" He stuck out from the crowd rather as the only person not wearing glasses.

"Course," Jerry said. "Let's go to the mobile."

In the mobile sat Stephen who looked up, shocked to see Wayno in the same room. He quickly got up and edged away.

"Can we have five minutes?" Jerry asked.

"Have as long as you want. I'm off to the library." Stephen grabbed his bag and skulked off looking back every now and then to check Jerry was okay.

Jerry looked at Wayno whose face hung forlornly beneath the still evident bruises and cuts.

"Sorry about the other night," Jerry muttered quickly.

"I dunno where the hell you suddenly appeared from but you saved my life." Wayno looked away out the window. "You do have some sort of superpowers don't you?"

"I wish." Jerry sat on a nearby desk. "What's going to happen to you now?"

"I'm staying with my grandparents." Wayno turned back towards Jerry. "My mum's mum and dad. They're really great. Dad'd never let me see them. They've been fighting ever since mum died."

"What about Bubbles?"

Wayno shook his head and looked away. After a moment he composed himself.

"But Nana and Gramps have said I can choose a puppy. Maybe something like a spaniel." The lad's mouth twisted into a wide smile.

"What's going to happen to your dad?"

"Dunno. Hope he rots in hell." Wayno turned away again.

"Must've been pretty hard on you, mate."

"Things used to be alright when Mum was around. She kept Dad calm. He used to hit her – she should've left him. Taken me away." Wayno's voice trembled and he stared out the window. "But she stayed with him until she got ill. He fell apart after that and life's been pretty crap ever since. You know, I never realised until now what a complete bastard I'd become. I'm really sorry, man."

Jerry allowed the long pause to engulf the overwhelming emotion. Wayno suddenly sniffed loudly and spun round.

"Hey today's good fun. You done well with all this stuff."

"So where are your specs then?"

Wayno sulkily put a hand in his blazer pocket and got out a grey case. Opening them awkwardly he carefully took out a pair of brown-rimmed NHS glasses and put them on.

"These are my real glasses – when I don't wear contacts."

"It's not very nice is it?"

"What?"

"Living in a world of myopia. It's not nice being short-sighted, although you've been incredibly short-sighted, blinkered and prejudiced for years."

"Huh?"

"You know you said I have superpowers? Well I don't." Jerry enjoyed the new power he had gained, but something inside made him feel sorry for Wayno.

"I think you do, man. You're a bloody superhero. I owe you

175

big time for helping me. I don't know how to repay you."

"You could stop being horrible to everyone." Jerry watched Wayno whose lips began to wiggle and twitch. "How about it?"

Wayno took off his glasses and wiped his eyes unselfconsciously, then nodded whilst biting his bottom lip. "Being short-sighted is pretty crap to know the truth."

"Could be worse," Jerry mused. "Sometimes it allows you to see the world from a slightly different perspective."

"I'm scared that one day I'll go blind."

"Remember that fear before you go around calling other people four-eyes, then."

Wayno sniffed and suppressed a cough. "I've learnt a hell of a lot recently. Now I'm away from my dad and with my Nana and Gramps I think things'll be very different."

Jerry held out a hand and to his surprise Wayno pulled him in for a big bear hug thumping his back a little too vehemently.

"You saved my life, man, and I'll never forget it. You're the dude!"

Before lunch ended he found Mindy. She ran up to him and grabbed him by the shoulders.

"I just heard what you did. You put yourself in danger. You idiot!"

Jerry was taken aback and tried to wriggle out of her grip. She only hung on tighter. He cast his eyes down to the ground.

"You could have been hurt, Jerry," she continued in a scolding tone. "There's a fine line between being a hero and being dead."

He felt her hand under his chin guiding his face up to hers. Her face brightened and before he knew it she kissed him on the lips.

"Lucky for you Jerry Hough, I think you're a complete hero.

Although you have a lot of making up to do before I completely forgive you."

A surprise awaited them on Wednesday. Miss Powys returned far sooner than they had anticipated. Vicki noticed the ring first.

"Ooh, miss, is that what I think it is?" she screeched as she ran to hug her form tutor. "Congratulations, miss. That's wicked innit?"

As all the girls crowded round her she smiled and held out her hand for their inspection.

"Yes it is what you're thinking. Alan asked me to marry him. It was so romantic."

"Oooh, please miss, tell us all about it."

The rumour about her being pregnant had somehow spread around. Jerry wondered how these things got out, as neither he nor Mindy had told anyone. Miss Powys had been anxious about gossip and rudeness but, to her delight, her situation seemed to make the pupils treat her with a new-found respect.

Whilst she happily recounted the joyous events surrounded by cooing girls, Jerry caught her eye and stuck his thumb up. She winked back at him as she continued the description of the restaurant and how Alan had got on one knee.

During registration that afternoon each member of the tutor group remained seated and answered their name with a quiet respect just as they had for Mr Finn. Miss Powys didn't reveal her surprise, but felt relieved that the old problems seemed to be gone, although she wondered how long it would last. She promised herself she'd enjoy it as long as it did. As the pupils filed out they all said goodbye in the friendliest of tones. Miss Powys clasped one hand over her bump and felt truly happy inside.

"I'm proud of the way things have turned out, Jerry," Mr Finn said at their daily meeting. "And I've some confidential news which I wanted to share with you."

"You know you can trust me, sir." Jerry sipped his coffee then put his cup down next to Mr Finn's basketball mug.

"Indeed I can." Mr Finn crossed his long legs narrowly missing kicking Jerry's shins. "You know the Headmaster has been ill for some time now, well he has just formally announced his retirement and the Governors are fully supporting my application for the post. They have to advertise of course and there will be external candidates so it's not a done deal, but I feel a certain confidence."

"They'd be stupid not to give you the job, sir."

"Thank you Jerry."

"In fact," Jerry added with a smile, "it would be very short-sighted of them."

Mr Finn snorted with laughter.

"Yes, some people do live in a world of myopia, Jerry. They don't see what we see do they? Their world is only full of haze and mistiness. People like you and me, on the other hand, have seen things normal-sighted people would never believe."

Jerry narrowed his eyes as he looked back at Mr Finn, who allowed his eyes to glaze slightly as if remembering something from his childhood.

"You see, most people think being myopic is a disability, but we know better don't we?" He turned to Jerry with a conspiratorial grin. "We know that it just gives us a slightly different perspective on life. I think you know what I mean." He stood up. "But now I have lots of work on so I'll see you later, Jerry."

"Thank you, sir."

Mr Finn opened the door for him and Jerry sauntered off down the corridor with a burning question in his mind.

Chapter Twenty-Two

It was a cool autumn morning when the new pupils arrived at school. Jerry was beginning year 11 and the teachers had drummed into them the importance of this final year and of working hard for their GCSEs.

In a corridor that led to a door to the outside field one overwhelmed year seven boy stood nervously alone under a staircase. Then he recognised a couple of other pupils from his form group moving towards him.

"Hello," he said, keen to make new friends.

The two boys looked at each other and grinned.

"Look who it is," said the one with floppy, forward-combed hair.

"Hey, it's Tarquin," replied the one with a shaved eyebrow. "Yo, Tarquin, you going to the library?" The two boys giggled.

"Or d'yaneed a wee-wee?" asked floppy hair. "I think the girls' loo is over there."

Shaved eyebrow gave floppy hair a high five before advanced menacingly again.

"Why are you such a little saddo, eh? Tarquin?"

"Repeat after me, 'I am a loser'."

"Yeah, you freak!"

Shaved eyebrow began to reach out to grab Tarquin's tie when he noticed the scared boy's eyes flick left to look past the two of them. But before shaved eyebrow could turn round he suddenly felt a strong arm round his neck.

"Leave the kid alone."

Floppy hair saw the older pupil grab his mate, but rather

than help out he gave a little yelp and ran off. Shaven eyebrow went helplessly limp, scared he'd stop breathing. The older pupil relaxed his grip and he nodded to Tarquin.

"Hold his shoulders, kid."

Tarquin nodded and did as he was told. Holding shaven eyebrow's shoulders as hard as he could, Tarquin then watched on delighted as the older pupil proceeded to debag the year seven bully. Just then a group of other children walked past and much merriment ensued as they pointed and howled with laughter at shaven eyebrow who fell to the floor and sorted himself out rapidly. As he tried to make his escape he was blocked by the older pupil.

"The name's Wayno. Remember it, kid. If I see you doing anything like that again then you have me to face. Understand?" Shaven eyebrow shook and nodded.

"Yeah, sorry." He was hoping it was enough to win his release but Wayno kept his grip on the scrawny year seven.

The crowd dispersed when they heard the sound of Quincy Finn OBE's voice.

"What's going on here then?"

Wayno faced Mr Finn, still holding shaven eyebrow, and smiled.

"Just some new pupils undergoing some essential education, sir."

"Ah, I see. Well good work, Cadman." Mr Finn peered at shaven eyebrow, committing his face to memory. "He'll soon learn the ropes, I'm sure."

Wayno released the boy who ran in the direction his friend had gone earlier.

"Well, I'll leave you to your good work then." Mr Finn executed a military about turn. "As you were Cadman."

Wayno and Tarquin watched the new Head Teacher continue on his tour of duty.

"The name's Wayno. Any trouble you find me or Jerry. What class you in?"

"7B sir," Tarquin stammered still reeling from the events of the last few moments.

"I'll come and collect you at lunchtime, okay?"

"Um, yeah, er, thanks."

"No probs, kid. Just doin' the right thing."

THE END

Fantastic Books
Great Authors

Meet our authors and discover our exciting range:

- Gripping Thrillers
- Cosy Mysteries
- Romantic Chick-Lit
- Fascinating Historicals
- Exciting Fantasy
- Young Adult and Children's Adventures

Visit us at:
www.crookedcatpublishing.com

Join us on facebook:
www.facebook.com/crookedcatpublishing